MW00945471

Hartley's Twisted Life

Kimberly Ann Purvis

Acknowledgements

I would like to thank my parents for their love and support and for always believing in me.

I am grateful to my editor, Kimberley Pinzon, for all her hard work.

Chapter 1

May 1981

It was a perfect day. No cloud dared to interrupt the beautiful sea of blue filling the sky. No one could possibly dream of the disaster that was about to strike.

* * * * * * * * * * * * * * * * * *

George Redfield sighed as he looked at the clock in the dashboard of the car. He had been driving for hours and was ready to get home. In the passenger's seat, his wife, Sarah, was sound asleep. In the backseat, their one-year-old daughter, Hartley, was wide awake in her car seat. George made a funny face in the rearview mirror, causing Hartley to giggle.

The Redfield family was returning home after spending the weekend in Topeka. George, a high-school science teacher, had spent the weekend at a required conference learning about the newest teaching methods. The conference was long and dull, but at least he was able to bring his family along. Sarah spent the day with Hartley at the zoo, and they had dinner together that night. Leaving around noon, George hoped to make the five hour drive to their home in Cainsville by nightfall, but traveling with a one-year-old could be unpredictable. Sarah's snores now filled the car. George looked at his wife, remembering the day they first met…

Sixteen-year-old George stepped out of the car and looked around the small town. The first thing that came to mind was Mayberry. There were old men sitting and talking outside the feed store. Children were riding their bikes down the middle of the street. Women were carrying bags full of groceries and stopping to gossip. George was secretly wondering if he had just made a terrible mistake.

"What do you think, son?" George's father, Ray asked from the driver's side of the car.

"It's different, Dad," was the only thing George could manage as he got out of the car to help his dad unload the boxes. George looked at the house his father had purchased. Just one block from the main street of Cainsville, it was a cheery blue two-story house complete with a white picket fence, very different from their house in San Francisco.

George's parents were recently divorced after twenty years of marriage. Ray, a doctor, was offered a job at the new Cainsville Community hospital. Wanting to get away from the city life, he accepted and moved to the tiny town on the Kansas/Oklahoma border. George wanted to try something new and decided to make the move with his dad. He loved his mom, Evelyn, and two-year-old brother, Bruce, but needed a change. George was starting to question that change - until he saw her.

She was sitting on the front porch reading a book. Her house was almost identical to George's but was yellow with bright red shutters. She had porcelain skin and long golden hair. George couldn't tell what color her eyes were, and he was very anxious to find out. George had never felt this way about a girl before. Back home, George was a loner and socially awkward. He wasn't athletic. George was smart, always making good grades, but did not possess the ability to be smooth like the popular kids at his school. It wasn't that he was bad looking, either. George was tall and lanky, with curly brown hair and dark blue eyes. He had just never had much luck with the ladies, but he was hoping that was about to change.

She must have sensed George's gawking, because she looked up and their eyes locked. She smiled and walked over to George. George discovered that she had beautiful green eyes.

"Hi," the girl said.

"Hello," George replied.

"I'm Sarah Hartley. I guess I'm your new neighbor." She said in a very soft, shy voice.

"Yeah, um, I'm George. George Redfield," George stuttered out. He held his hand out for her to shake but dropped the box he was holding in the process. George sighed at his clumsiness.

Sarah laughed and said, "Let me help." Together they picked up the contents of the box.

"So, you moved from San Francisco, right? Your dad's the new doctor?" Sarah asked as she handed the box to George.

"Yeah, how did you know that?" George asked curiously. Maybe Sarah was psychic.

"Cainsville is a very small town. Everybody knows everything. You'll get used to it" Sarah said.

"Wow, it's really different from California. I didn't even know our old neighbors." George said.

"Do you need some help with those?" Sarah asked pointing to the many boxes.

"No, you don't have to." George started to say, but Sarah had already grabbed a box and was walking towards the house.

"So do you have any brothers and sisters?" Sarah asked. *Apparently the town didn't know everything about them yet* thought George.

"I have a brother, Bruce. He lives with our mom." George explained.

"I have a sister. We're twins. You'll meet her at school tomorrow." Sarah said as they continued to unload boxes.

"I'll just look for the girl that looks like you." George said.

"No" Sarah said shaking her head. "Laura and I look nothing alike. She has red hair, freckles, and blue eyes."

"So much for the twin thing, huh?" George said.

"We don't really act alike either. Our mom says she would be worried we weren't twins if we hadn't come out at the same time." Sarah said.

When they had finished unloading everything, George introduced Sarah to his dad. George and Sarah walked outside together. Sarah was pointing everything out.

"My parents own the feed store," she explained. "The Williams live across the street there. They're really nice, but watch out for their son, Randy. He likes to throw rocks at people. Just threaten to tell his dad, and he'll leave you alone."

"Thanks for everything," George said not wanting to say goodbye to Sarah.

"You're welcome. I'll see you at school tomorrow. Do you know what classes you're taking yet?" She asked.

"No. I don't know." George said, hoping that he would be in Sarah's class.

"You seem smart. You'll probably be in the advanced classes with me. But if they put you in the regular classes, don't worry, you'll be in same class

9

with Laura." Sarah said as she waved goodbye and went into her house. George sighed as he realized he was in love with the girl next door and was suddenly very happy that he had decided to move to Kansas.

The next day as he enrolled in Cainsville High School, he made a point to ask to be in the advanced classes. George met with Principal Dill who seemed nice and answered all of George's questions. The secretaries were also very pleasant and seemed excited to have someone new at the school. George got the feeling that Cainsville didn't get new students often.

Talking to the principal made George late for his first class. Since he was already late, George decided to stop by his locker and drop off some of the heavy books he received in the office. When he finally located his locker, he found that it wouldn't open. George pulled with all his might but couldn't get the door to budge.

"You have to kick it," a voice from behind told George. George turned to see a boy halfway hiding behind a wall. He was a few inches shorter than George but more muscular. He had sandy blond hair and brown eyes. He was wearing a red letterman jacket.

"What?" George asked.

"You have to kick the door to open it, but I wouldn't if I were you," the hidden boy informed George.

"Why shouldn't I open it?" George asked. He wondered if the students had filled it with garbage or something, trying to play a prank on the new kid.

"It was Stinky McGee's locker. He used to keep his sweaty gym clothes in there. He left but the smell didn't," he told George as he continued to hide.

George decided to take a chance and kicked the door. Sure enough, it swung open and a horrible smell bombarded George. He quickly dropped his books inside and slammed the door shut.

"I told you," the boy said.

"What are you doing?" George asked.

"Making sure the coast is clear," the boy said. "I'm Wyatt by the way. Wyatt Sawyer."

"I'm George Redfield," George introduced himself but was cut off by Wyatt.

"I know who you are. The whole school does." Wyatt said as he continued to make sure the coast was clear. "The joys of small town living, everyone knows everything about you already."

"It's definitely different," George simply said.

"Don't worry - you'll get used to it - I did. I moved here from Dallas a couple of years ago," Wyatt said.

George just nodded in response and realized he should be getting to class.

"Hey, could you give me hand with these?" Wyatt said. George stepped around the corner to see what he was pointing to. George saw four large buckets filled with some sort of yellow substance.

"I would like to, but I really should be getting to class," George said.

"What class do you have?" Wyatt asked.

"History," George answered.

"You don't want to be in there right now. Mr. Malone's teaching about the Revolutionary War which will lead to him having one of his war flashbacks. It gets really messy. Trust me. He won't notice you didn't show up," Wyatt informed him.

"Alright," George said reluctantly. He had no idea if he should trust Wyatt, but he was the first student he met that day. He couldn't be that bad of guy, could he?

"What is this?" George asked curiously as he picked up two of the buckets and followed Wyatt down the deserted hallway.

"Twenty four gallons of cream corn," Wyatt said proudly.

"Okay," George said slowly. "Why do you need twenty four gallons of cream corn?"

"I'm going to put it in Principal Dill's car," Wyatt said.

"Why?" George said as he struggled to carry the buckets. Cream corn was surprisingly heavy.

"Because he suspended me from playing in the football game Friday night. I'm the quarterback, and the team needs me," Wyatt explained.

"Why did he do that?" George asked, now thinking it probably wasn't a good idea for him to be an accomplice in this plan.

"Because of the goat thing," Wyatt said.

"What goat thing?" George asked curiously.

"I stole a goat and put in his office," Wyatt bragged.

"And they didn't kick you out of school for that?" George asked. At George's old school he would have been kicked out in a blink of an eye.

"No. There's a 'three strikes and you're out' rule here. That was only my second strike," Wyatt boasted.

"Should I even ask what the first strike was?" George said.

"Probably not," Wyatt replied with a smile.

They had almost made it to the door when they heard someone cough behind them. They slowly turned to see Principal Dill.

"Step into my office boys," Principal Dill said.

13

* * * * * * * * * * * * * * * * * * *

"George, I can't help but feel this is my fault," Wyatt said.

"You don't say," George muttered as he frowned at Wyatt. They were the only students in detention that day. The old teacher in charge, whose name George couldn't remember, was reading a book and not paying them any attention. Wyatt mentioned that he was deaf in one ear.

George's first day of school was not going as planned. The day started off with getting an afternoon of detention. The whole school seemed to think George was a troublemaker. The only bright spot to George's day was being in the same class as Sarah. George prayed that Sarah didn't think of him that way.

"Come on, it's not like it's your first time in detention," Wyatt said.

George didn't say a word. His perfect school record was gone, no thanks to Wyatt.

"Really? Your first detention? I feel honored, George."

George just glared at him.

"Don't worry I have a plan to get us out of here." Wyatt informed him.

Before George could ask what the plan was, a girl with wild curly red hair came stomping into the room. She was wearing a cheerleading outfit and a very angry expression.

"Wyatt Sawyer, how could you!" the girl screeched so loudly even the half-deaf teacher paid attention.

"What's wrong, baby?" Wyatt asked smoothly.

"Don't you baby me. You know what you did," the girl yelled.

"Miss Hartley, I'm afraid, you can't be in here," the teacher decided to intervene.

Hartley? That must be Sarah's sister, Laura, thought George. Sarah was right; they really didn't look anything alike.

However, Laura paid no attention to the teacher. She continued ranting at Wyatt.

"You were supposed to drive me home. Instead you get yourself thrown into detention again!" Laura screamed. "I bet you don't even know what today is!"

"Your birthday?" Wyatt guessed.

Smack! Laura had slapped Wyatt across the face. At this move, the teacher got up from his desk and began dragging Laura out the door who was still screaming at Wyatt.

"It's our anniversary!" She yelled as the teacher was still pulling her out the door.

George heard the teacher begin lecturing her outside.

15

"Time to go," Wyatt said to George. George turned to see Wyatt opening a window.

"We'll get in more trouble," George tried to reason with Wyatt.

"No we won't," Wyatt assured him. George decided to follow him if only because he didn't want to explain where Wyatt was when the teacher returned. They jumped out the window and began to run and didn't stop until they reached the gym.

George was about to ask if the teacher would be looking for them when Laura ran around the corner, jumped into Wyatt's arms, and began kissing him. When she noticed George, the two separated.

"Hi! You must be George. Wow, Sarah was right about you. You are cute." Laura said. George blushed at this comment but was delighted to hear Sarah thought he was cute.

"Are you trying to trade me in?" Wyatt asked jokingly.

"Of course not, baby! He's too dorky for me." Laura said. George didn't know if he should be offended or not until Laura added, "He's perfect for Sarah, though." George was thrilled by that news.

Before George could respond, he saw horrified looks appear on Wyatt's and Laura's faces. They were staring at something just behind him. He turned to see Principal Dill.

"This is the final straw, Mr. Sawyer. I've had enough of your troublemaking. This is your third strike. You are suspended," Principal Dill said firmly.

"But," Wyatt opened his mouth to protest, but George cut him off.

"It was my idea, sir," George admitted.

"That's very nice of you to defend your friend, Mr. Redfield, but completely unnecessary," Principal Dill replied.

"It really was my idea. I used to do this all the time at my old school. I talked them into it," George admitted.

The principal took a minute to look at the other two. They shook their head in agreement with George.

"Very well, Mr. Redfield. You'll be serving two weeks of detention, and I'll have my eye on you. Mr. Sawyer, one more strike and you *will* be expelled," Principal Dill threatened and then walked away.

Wyatt and Laura waited until the principal was out of earshot to begin thanking George.

"That was so nice, thank you," Laura said, hugging George.

"George, you saved my life, thank you," Wyatt said, also giving George a hug.

When they finished hugging George, Wyatt said, "If you need anything, I owe you one."

George thought about this for a moment and then replied, "There is one thing you can do for me."

"Name it," Wyatt said.

"Both of you can help me get a date with Sarah," George said.

Wyatt and Laura looked at each other and smiled. George smiled back at them, having no idea what he was getting himself into.

* * * * * * * * * * * * * * * * * *

Two years later, they graduated. George managed to convince his best friend, Wyatt, to get enough school credit to graduate and to tame his troublemaking habits. Wyatt and Laura managed to get George the girl of his dreams. Laura and Wyatt were still together which surprised everyone, while George and Sarah had been inseparable for two years.

George was the salutatorian and Sarah was the valedictorian. They had both been accepted to Stanford University. George was excited to return to California, especially with Sarah. Wyatt and Laura's grades were too low for college. Wyatt astonished everyone when he joined the army. He also astonished everyone by proposing to Laura. There was a quick and outrageous wedding in Las

Vegas. George was the best man while Sarah was the maid of honor.

As Wyatt prepared to leave for basic training, Laura and Sarah prepared to be separated for the first time in eighteen years. George knew it would be hard for Sarah, so he did everything to make the transition as easy as possible for her. The two couples said goodbye and embarked on new journeys.

Four years later, George and Sarah graduated from college. George graduated with a Chemistry degree and Sarah graduated with an English degree. Even though they loved California, George knew Sarah wanted to go home to Kansas. After two tours of duty, Wyatt was honorably discharged from the army. Wyatt and Laura moved into Wyatt's grandparent's farmhouse on the outskirts of Cainsville, which he had inherited after his grandfather died.

George and Sarah were married shortly after their college graduation. Instead of running off to Vegas, they opted for a quaint church wedding with family and friends. Wyatt was the best man; Laura was the matron of honor. They accepted teaching jobs at their old high school. Ray received a new job in Detroit and gave the happy couple a great wedding present, his house in Cainsville.

From the very first day, George and Sarah loved married life. They also loved working together. They didn't think life could get any better until they learned they were expecting. It was the happiest day of both George and Sarah's lives when they welcomed Hartley Ray Redfield into the world. Sarah quit her job to be a stay-at-home mom. George and Sarah loved Hartley more than anything in the world. Aunt Laura and Uncle Wyatt were just as smitten with Hartley. Together the two couples enjoyed spoiling the infant as much as possible.

Chapter 2

George shook his head to clear his mind of the happy memories. He loved to reminisce about his courtship with Sarah, but he needed to remain alert as he drove home.

George smiled as he recalled his courtship and glanced at the curly haired blonde in the backseat. Hartley let out another giggle, this time waking her mother.

"What are you two doing?" asked Sarah in a sleepy voice.

"Oh, nothing, Hartley was just being funny" replied George.

"Were you making daddy laugh, silly baby?" Sarah asked Hartley as she reached around to tickle her. Hartley giggled even louder, causing her parents to laugh with her.

"How much longer, sweetheart?" Sarah asked George after they both calmed down from laughing.

"About thirty more miles and we should be home." George said.

By that time it was 5:30 p.m. George noticed that the beautiful sunny sky had disappeared and been replaced with a dark, ominous one. The highway was completely deserted. No other cars had passed them for miles, and the sky appeared to be worsening. Sarah seemed to read George's mind.

"Why don't you turn on the radio and see if there are any weather reports." Sarah told George. The one thing George missed about California was the weather. Kansas weather was completely unpredictable.

George had originally turned the radio off so Sarah could sleep peacefully. The radio announcer's voice filled the car. "The National Weather Service has issued a tornado warning for the following counties…." The announcer named at least eleven counties including the one they were currently in.

Living in the middle of Tornado Alley, tornado warnings were common. Usually when the warnings were issued, George, Sarah, and Hartley would seek shelter in the safety of their basement.

"I'm worried, George. The weather looks really bad." Sarah said with a concerned look on her face.

"We'll be fine, don't worry. We'll make it home before the storm hits." George replied, although he was worried too. He had not seen a house for miles. They were surrounded by deserted plains. If a tornado did hit, they were completely exposed.

"We'll be home soon." George told Sarah.

At that moment, a massive, swirling, black cloud descended from the sky. The twister was only three miles in front of the car. George slammed on the brakes and made a sharp U-turn in the middle of the highway. He smashed the accelerator, but it was no use. The car was no match for the winds from the tornado, sucking the car backwards into the mass of darkness. The glass of the windshield and windows shattered as the tornado's winds roared. All George could hear was Sarah's screams and Hartley's cries. "Please don't take Hartley. She's too young. Please don't let her die like this." George silently prayed.

"I love you" Sarah screamed to George and Hartley. She too sent up a silent prayer, begging God to let her baby live.

"I love you both" were the last words that George Redfield would ever speak as the twister completely engulfed the car.

* * * * * * * * * * * * * * * * * * * *

Sheriff Jerry Jackson was in his car, patrolling the town and seeing the damage the twister had caused when he got the call.

"Everyone is accounted for in the town, Sheriff, except the Redfields. Laura Sawyer just called the station. She sounded pretty worried. She said she hasn't heard from them and they should have made it back by now."

"I'll check the county and see if I can find them." Sheriff Jackson radioed back to the station.

The twister had left the town of Cainsville in terrible condition. Most towns didn't survive large tornadoes like the one that had just ripped through. There had been a few injuries but no fatalities. The twister had narrowly missed wiping out Cainsville. The Sheriff hoped the Redfields hadn't been caught in the twister. He was a friend of theirs and silently prayed for their safety.

The Sheriff had reached Harper's field, located about thirty miles outside of Cainsville, when he saw the car, or rather, the remnants of a car. He radioed the station telling them to send an ambulance right away. As he drove closer to the scene, he realized there was no use.

He found George and Sarah's bodies inside the car. Barely holding back the tears, the Sheriff took a deep breath as he looked in the back seat. Expecting to see the body of baby Hartley, he was surprised to find an empty back seat. He knew the body must be in the field somewhere, so he started searching. He had his flashlight out and was shuffling through the debris when he heard something in the distance. A faint cry was ringing out in the darkness. The sheriff froze. There was no way Hartley Redfield could have survived the deadly twister. He heard the cry again and started sprinting in its direction.

He found her about a hundred yards from where the car lay destroyed. She was lying on the ground and covered in dirt. The sheriff carefully picked Hartley up, in case she was injured. As he held the crying baby in his arms he realized with shock that she was completely fine.

By that time, the ambulance along with Wyatt and Laura Sawyer had arrived. Upon seeing the bodies of her twin sister and brother-in-law, Laura fell to the ground screaming hysterically. Wyatt tried to comfort his wife but could barely control his own tears.

As they watched the bodies being pulled from the car, Wyatt asked, "Where's Hartley?"

"Over here!" the sheriff shouted, carefully carrying Hartley in his arms.

Laura and Wyatt ran toward the sheriff.

"Is she okay?" Laura asked as tears ran down her face.

"She seems perfectly fine. Better let the paramedics look at her to be sure" the Sheriff told them as he gently placed Hartley in Laura's arms.

"Oh, thank God!" Laura said as she hugged Hartley tightly. Wyatt kissed the baby on the forehead as she drifted off to sleep.

"How did she survive that?" Wyatt asked what seemed to be on everyone's mind.

"Must be a miracle" the Sheriff said. "I've never seen anything like this. You have a very special baby right there."

They all looked down at the infant. None of them could possibly know how special Hartley Ray Redfield truly was or the abilities that the twister had bestowed upon her.

Chapter 3

"BEEP! BEEP! BEEP!" The sound of the alarm clock roused Hartley from a deep sleep. She had been dreaming about a tornado again.

"AGH!!" Hartley yelled as she rolled out of bed and onto the floor, missing the button to turn off her annoying alarm clock. Landing with a thud on the hardwood floor of her bedroom, Hartley heard a bark from above. Looking up, Hartley saw the furry face of her golden retriever, Bob Dylan, curiously looking down at her from the foot of her bed. His facial expression seemed to say it all, asking why she had so rudely disrupted his sleep.

"I know, Bob, I know. I'm sorry." Hartley apologized to the dog, as she tried to disentangle her leg from the quilt it was wrapped in.

Hartley glared angrily at the alarm clock, the source of her problems, which read 7:35 a.m.

"I'm late for school!" Hartley yelled causing Bob Dylan to bark again.

Hartley was never late. This was not a good way to start the day.

Running to her closet, Hartley grabbed the first thing she could find and ran toward the bathroom. She quickly threw on a red sundress with

27

yellow daisies, a denim jacket, and cowboy boots, all of which were staples in her wardrobe. She tried to run a brush through the tangled mess she called hair, but it didn't seem to work. She threw it in a ponytail and silently rebuked herself for sleeping with wet hair again. As she dabbed on her makeup, Hartley studied her reflection in the mirror. She liked to play a stupid game were she matched her features to her parents. In a weird way it made Hartley feel closer to them, being able to see them in her own face.

She had her mother's porcelain skin and green eyes. Hartley had her father's curly hair, nose and dimple in her chin. Her hair was a blend of both parents, resulting in a dark blonde color. She was the same height as her mother. She knew this because she was the same height as her Aunt Laura. Hartley had a soft body, not athletic. She was a healthy weight because she refused to starve herself like the anorexic girls at her school.

She made it downstairs by 7:45. School started at 8:00 sharp. Aunt Laura and Uncle Wyatt were eating breakfast at the kitchen table as Hartley sprinted past them.

"Slow down, Hartley, you're going to hurt yourself," Uncle Wyatt cautioned. Her aunt and uncle were both aware of how clumsy and uncoordinated she was.

"I overslept, and now I'm late for school!" Hartley yelled as she tried to gather all her books and notebooks that were scattered across the kitchen.

"It's not the end of the world if you're a few minutes late for school. Heck, I once missed an entire month of school and they still let me graduate," Uncle Wyatt said proudly. Of course, Uncle Wyatt had been a slacker in high school and didn't go to college. Hartley didn't take time to point this out, but made a mental note that punctuality was a key to success.

"I have perfect attendance, and if I'm late it will mess everything up," Hartley replied. She thought she heard Uncle Wyatt cough "dork" under his breath, but she didn't have time to deal with that now.

"Hartley, you can't go to school without eating breakfast. It's not healthy," Aunt Laura told her.

"I don't have time to eat, Aunt Laura. I have to get to school," Hartley insisted.

"Well, eat this," Aunt Laura said placing a piece of toast smothered in jam in Hartley's mouth. Hartley's hands were currently full of books as she was trying to stuff them in her book bag.

"Thank you," muffled Hartley as she headed for the door.

"Wait, you forgot your lunch!" Aunt Laura called after her.

Hartley made a quick turn and grabbed the brown paper bag from her aunt.

"I made your favorite, chicken salad," Aunt Laura smiled as she handed Hartley the bag and kissed her on the forehead.

"Come home right after school, Hartley, I need your help with the old tractor. It won't crank again," Uncle Wyatt called out after her. "And have a good day at school."

"Okay. I will. Love you. Bye!" Hartley shouted at her aunt and uncle as she ran to her truck.

Her Aunt Laura and Uncle Wyatt were the best substitute parents anyone could have asked for. Although they favored a laid-back parenting style which included being far too lenient with the rules, this wasn't hard for Hartley, who took rules seriously. They loved her like she supposed her parents would have. Hartley knew her aunt and uncle considered her their own daughter, probably because they were never able to have their own children. Hartley also knew her aunt and uncle truly loved her because they never treated her like a freak for being a little different than most kids.

Hartley got into her 1967 baby-blue Chevy truck. The truck had once belonged to Uncle Wyatt's grandfather. Uncle Wyatt had been raised by his grandparents and was given the truck on his sixteenth birthday. Uncle Wyatt gave it to Hartley on her sixteenth birthday. Hartley knew they could not afford a new car. She knew her aunt and uncle were not rich. They always gave her the best they could afford, and that was perfectly fine with Hartley. The little money her parents had was currently in a savings account for Hartley's college tuition.

Hartley turned the truck onto the highway. School was a fifteen minute drive, and if she made good time, she might avoid being tardy. Her truck refused to go over the speed limit. She looked at her reflection in the rearview mirror. Her face gave no indication that there was anything unusual about her.

Hartley had a special "gift". She had the ability to see where future tornadoes were going to hit. Ever since she could remember, Hartley had visions of tornadoes. Once when she was three years old, she had hidden in the basement. When Aunt Laura and Uncle Wyatt found her, they asked what she was doing. She replied, "Hiding from the tornado." One minute later a tornado hit. That's when they realized something was different about Hartley.

The visions were always different, usually singling out a specific person. Whether it was a classmate, or a citizen of Cainsville, Hartley would see a tornado hurting or killing that person. Her visions were very intense and horribly graphic. It wasn't uncommon for Hartley to get sick after "seeing" someone she knew die. But this only motivated her more to save whoever she saw in her visions.

In third grade, she locked one of her classmates, Chesney, in the bathroom after school, ensuring that he would miss the bus. Finally, his parents came looking for him, guaranteeing that they were all out of the house when a tornado destroyed their home that afternoon. In ninth grade, Hartley had a vision of a tornado hitting the school. She told her teacher she was sick and needed to go to the nurse's office, conveniently located in the main office. When she got to the main office, she told the school secretary that the two kids were fighting down the hall. While the unsuspecting secretaries ran down the hall looking for the kids, Hartley pulled the alarm signaling a tornado, and the whole school was able to get to safety.

Just last month, Hartley had prevented her favorite teacher, Mr. Pooler, from a tornado disaster. In her vision, Hartley had seen Mr. Pooler drive off a bridge, trying to turn around after a tornado descending from the sky. Hartley had watched in horror as Mr. Pooler, unable to escape from his car, drowned. Hartley knew Mr. Pooler stayed late after school to grade papers. In the vacant school parking lot, she took the spark plugs out of his car, stranding him at school and ensuring his safety.

Hartley only had visions of tornadoes. She never had visions of hurricanes, earthquakes, snowstorms, or any other type of natural disaster. She only saw tornadoes. Once, Hartley had been visiting her Grandma Evelyn in San Francisco when a minor earthquake hit. She had no idea an earthquake was going to happen. Last winter, a blizzard buried the entire Midwest, including Kansas, in several feet of snow. Hartley had no idea that it was going to hit.

Hartley often had to create crazy plans to help people. Hartley wasn't proud of the fact that she sometimes had to commit illegal acts to guarantee people's safety. She justified her actions by telling herself it was for her safety, too. Hartley knew if anyone ever found out about her ability, they would think she was crazy.

No one except Aunt Laura and Uncle Wyatt knew about Hartley's talent. They wanted to take Hartley to a specialist when she was little to make sure she wasn't crazy. But fearful the doctors would have her committed, they decided against it. How could she be crazy if the visions were true? Every time she predicted a tornado, one would strike. Aunt Laura and Uncle Wyatt decided to keep Hartley's gift a secret and to help her whenever she needed.

Besides, every year at her annual checkup, the doctor said Hartley was perfectly healthy.

Hartley turned into the school parking lot. Cainsville High School was not hard to find, considering the small size of the town. The high school was so small that, combined with the elementary and middle school, there were just four hundred and twelve students. The senior class only had twenty-one students. Hartley searched the small parking lot, which the students shared with the faculty, for a parking space. The cars and trucks that filled the lot were old and used. Cainsville was a farming community and not many people had the money for new cars. Hartley's truck fit right in with the others.

With a stroke of luck, Hartley spotted an empty space near the entrance. Just as she was about to pull into the spot, a red BMW convertible whipped into the space instead. Hartley knew all too well who the car belonged to, the one person in the world Hartley couldn't stand, Carmen Guilden.

Carmen Guilden was the stepdaughter of the mayor of Cainsville, and in Hartley's opinion a completely heinous human being. Carmen's mother, Camille, married Mayor Frank Guilden a few years ago. The Mayor was a very rich man. He was a part of the Guilden family that founded Cainsville over one hundred and twenty years ago. The family owned half the land and businesses in Cainsville.

Many of the businesses and land they had acquired through shady business deals. They were not a family to anger. Hartley suspected the mayor had only been elected to office by buying votes.

The Mayor was notorious for collecting trophy wives. Each time he remarried, the wife got younger. Camille was no exception. She was thirty years younger than the sixty-six year old mayor. Hartley had hoped this marriage wouldn't last long, but unfortunately it seemed the fourth time was the charm. The mayor, who never had children, adopted Carmen as a sign of his strong commitment to his new marriage.

Carmen arrived at Cainsville during ninth grade. Hartley had tried to be nice and friendly to the new kid, but Carmen wanted no part of it. From the first day that they met, Carmen had been nothing but cruel to Hartley. It seemed Carmen only wanted to make Hartley's life a nightmare, a hobby at which she excelled. Carmen instantly became popular based on her looks and money. Everyone knew not to trouble the mayor, especially his new daughter.

Carmen reminded Hartley of a Barbie doll: shiny and fake. Everything about Carmen was unnatural. She had fake, bleach-blonde hair. She wore contacts so her dark eyes could be blue. She got a spray tan every few weeks to keep her skin dark year round. For her sixteenth birthday, the mayor paid for Carmen's plastic surgery. Her nose became slimmer and her chest became larger. She was naturally tall, but in the five inch heels she wore every day she towered over six feet. Carmen was constantly on a diet to stay at the perfect size zero. She was a younger replica of her mother. Hartley figured Carmen would one day follow in her mother's footsteps and marry for money.

During her first year at Cainsville High, Carmen teased Hartley for being smart. As the year progressed, so did Carmen's teasing. Carmen teased Hartley for being ugly. Carmen teased Hartley for being poor. Carmen teased Hartley for being an orphan. Carmen teased Hartley for not being popular. Carmen teased Hartley for anything and everything. In the tenth and eleventh grade, Carmen's torture evolved into pretending Hartley didn't exist. She completely ignored her presence. She even got most of the school to do the same thing. Hartley hated the feeling of being invisible. Finally, during their senior year, Carmen had decided just to hurt Hartley whenever she pleased.

Hartley could handle the teasing most of time. She would often vent to her aunt and uncle, who encouraged her to be the bigger person. Mostly Hartley hated the way Carmen made her feel about herself. High school was hard enough. If Hartley ever had self-esteem, Carmen had destroyed it years ago. Hartley frequently found herself fantasizing about a tornado whisking Carmen far away, but her daydreams never came true.

That morning as Carmen stepped out of her car, Hartley revved the engine of truck, pretending she was going to run over Carmen. Carmen was so surprised that she tripped and fell flat on the ground. Hartley couldn't control her laughing as she watched Carmen struggle to stand up in her high heels. Carmen shot Hartley one of her nastiest glares as she went inside. If looks could kill, Hartley would be dead. Hartley set out in search of another parking spot. Finding one at the very end of the parking lot, Hartley had to sprint in hopes of making it to class on time.

Hartley's first class was Calculus. Although she despised it, Hartley was an okay math student. She much preferred her science and English classes. Another reason for her hatred towards Calculus was her evil teacher, Mr. Mercer. Mr. Mercer was a grouchy old man who believed in being very strict and difficult. He seemed to have a special hatred for his students. He loved to give people detention. Hartley, fortunately, had a perfect record, with no detentions. She knew if she was late for class, Mr. Mercer would be happy to destroy that perfect record.

Hartley sprinted down the hall to class. She made it into her desk, located in the very back of the classroom, just as the bell rang. Mr. Mercer was already writing what looked like a very complex problem on the board. Hartley took out her notebook and began working. After writing the problem down, Hartley started to gaze around the room. She saw Carmen had made it to class and had taken her usual spot next to her boyfriend, Tyler Heath. Hartley's heart started beating faster as Tyler looked up and saw her gawking. He smiled at her and went back to working. Hartley quickly did the same thing.

Tyler Heath was Hartley's next door neighbor and the boy she had been in love with her entire life. Tyler's family owned the farm next to the Sawyers. Tyler and Hartley had always known each other. They had once been best friends, but that changed when Carmen arrived in Cainsville. Carmen had instantly set her sights on Tyler. They had been dating on and off again for the last few years. They were in a constant cycle of breaking up and getting back together. Hartley couldn't understand their relationship and decided it was best if she didn't try.

Hartley glanced back at Tyler. He had the All-American boy good looks. He was tall, with thick dark hair and brilliant blue eyes. Tyler reminded Hartley of a young superman. Tyler was talented, too. He was the star of the baseball team; in fact, he had already received a baseball scholarship from the University of Oklahoma.

Hartley didn't care about any of this, though. She loved how kind and thoughtful Tyler was, not a quality found in most of the teenage boys she knew.

Hartley returned her focus to the chalkboard. Mr. Mercer was rapidly explaining that the best way to solve the problem was with a new formula. Hartley was in the middle of trying the new formula when the vision started.

The gruesome black tornado was at least a mile wide. Hartley had never seen a twister of its size. It was traveling very fast and gaining on Hartley who was watching the scene from her rearview mirror. She heard a loud screaming coming from the passenger's seat of her truck. As she began to turn her head to see who was screaming, she heard someone calling her name.

"Miss Redfield" she heard the voice say. She was slowly coming out of her vision. "Miss Redfield" the same voice repeated, gradually becoming louder. Finally she heard the same voice shout, "MISS REDFIELD!!" followed by a loud thumping of someone slamming his hand on her desk.

Hartley sat straight up, her heart pounding. Slightly confused, she looked around the room and realized she was still in her Calculus class. Mr. Mercer was standing next to her desk, wearing a very angry expression.

"Miss Redfield, how nice of you to join the class," said Mr. Mercer. "Since you are so intelligent and no longer need to stay conscious for my class, maybe you would be so kind and help Mr. Heath solve the problem on the board?"

"What??" was the only thing Hartley could manage to say. She looked over to Tyler, who was sending her a look, begging for help.

"The answer to the problem, Miss Redfield," Mr. Mercer repeated.

Hartley looked at the board and thankfully realized she already had the correct answer.

"Negative four," replied Hartley.

Mr. Mercer seemed startled that she had answered the problem correctly. He quickly recovered from his shock and turned his focus back to his attack on Tyler.

"Well, Mr. Heath, your grade in this class continues to be miserable, and it seems that you could learn a few things from Miss Redfield. So as of today, Miss Redfield you will be Mr. Heath's tutor," said Mr. Mercer.

"But…" Hartley and Tyler both started to retaliate but Mr. Mercer cut them off. "Or perhaps both of you would like to spend the rest of the week in detention?"

"For what?" Tyler asked angrily.

"For failing to have the correct answer every time I ask you a question and for your unnecessary attitude, Mr. Heath," Mr. Mercer shouted at Tyler then turned to Hartley and said, "and for thinking so highly of yourself that you feel it is okay to sleep in my class."

Both Tyler and Hartley sat in silence, fuming over Mr. Mercer's words. The rest of the class watched in amazement. It was the first time they knew of that a teacher was yelling at Hartley Redfield.

"Now I take your silence to mean that neither of you wants detention, am I correct?" Mr. Mercer asked the two. Both Hartley and Tyler nodded their heads solemnly.

"If Mr. Heath's grade does not improve, Miss Redfield, I am going to assume that you are not taking your job seriously or that Mr. Heath is not taking his studies seriously. When that happens, I am going to give both of you detention for the remainder of the school year. Do I make myself clear?" asked Mr. Mercer, daring one of them to cross him again.

"Yes, sir," was all Hartley could say. Tyler just nodded, not trusting himself to speak again.

Thankfully the bell rang, and Mr. Mercer hastily assigned a ridiculous amount of homework for the night. He told the class to thank Tyler and Hartley for it. The class grumbled in complaint and began filing out of the classroom, Hartley in the lead. Feeling a mixture of embarrassment and anger, Hartley did not want to spend another minute in Mr. Mercer's classroom.

She was making her way to her locker down the hall, when in the corner of her eye, she saw Tyler appear beside her.

"Can you believe that? All because I didn't know one answer. Everyone already knows I'm stupid. And who cares if you sleep through class? You could sleep through every class and still ace them!" Tyler ranted as he walked perfectly in stride with Hartley.

"Calm down, Tyler, you don't want Mr. Mercer to give you detention for ranting in the hallway," replied Hartley remembering how easy it was for her to talk to Tyler. She looked over and saw that Tyler was smiling. "You're not stupid. Calculus is hard for everybody, and Mr. Mercer just makes it worse."

"You don't have to tutor me, Hartley, I'll figure it out on my own." Tyler said.

"Are you kidding me? I'm not risking ruining my perfect permanent record with a month's worth of detentions. We'll start today," Hartley informed him.

"Okay, if you insist. I have baseball practice, so how about five?" asked Tyler.

"That's fine," said Hartley as they reached her locker.

"My house?" asked Tyler.

"Sure," Hartley answered.

"Thanks, Hartley, you're the best," Tyler said as he walked away.

"If I'm the best, then why am I not your girlfriend?" thought Hartley. Hartley mentally reprimanded herself. She calmly explained to herself that she didn't need a boyfriend. High school was almost over. She never had a boyfriend before, and she didn't need one now. *"You'll get one in college or after college. You do not need a man. You are a strong, independent and intelligent girl who does not need a boyfriend."* Hartley chanted mentally.

In spite of her chant, Hartley knew that if she were being honest with herself, she would like to have a boyfriend. Especially the one she was just talking to, but he had his Barbie doll girlfriend. Hartley was out of luck. Aunt Laura was always reassuring Hartley that she was just a late bloomer and "her time would come", but Hartley had her doubts. Her parents met in high school. So had her aunt and uncle. What if she had already missed her chance?

During this mental pep talk, Hartley had been trying in vain to open her locker door. It was old and refused to open on a regular basis. She tugged with all her might, and the door flew open, hitting her in the middle of her forehead.

"Ouch!" cried Hartley, dropping all her books to the floor and clutching her forehead in pain.

"Smooth move," came a voice from behind, belonging to Hartley's best friend, Keisha Barnes.

"This is not my day," replied Hartley, still holding on to her head which was now throbbing.

"So I heard," said Keisha, picking up Hartley's books for her.

"How could you have possibly heard about it already? You're not even in my class," replied Hartley, looking curiously at her best friend. As there were only twenty-one students in the senior class, they were divided into two groups of ten students and eleven students. Hartley was in the class of eleven students that had Calculus first period, while Keisha was in the class of ten that had British Literature first period. Keisha always knew what was going on at school. She had a real talent for knowing everybody's business that Hartley genuinely admired.

Hartley and Keisha became friends two years ago when Keisha moved to Cainsville from Chicago with her mom. Hartley remembered their first meeting like it was yesterday...

Sixteen year old Hartley had been standing in the office getting a note for being absent from her first class. She had been at the orthodontist finally getting the braces she had been wearing for the past three years removed. She was waiting for Mrs. Phillips to sign her note when Hartley saw Keisha and her mother leave the Principal's office talking to Principal Burns. Keisha was a cute, short, black girl, with wildly curly hair.

"Oh, Hartley, I'd like you to meet our new student, Keisha Barnes." Principal Burns said. He turned to Mrs. Barnes and said, "Hartley is one of our best students. She's also in the tenth grade. I'm sure she would be glad to show Keisha around." Principal Burns gave Hartley a look, telling her she had no choice.

"I'd be happy to," Hartley said. Keisha, however, did not seem happy at all.

Hartley led Keisha around school, showing her where everything was. She tried, unsuccessfully to make small talk.

"So where did you move from?" Hartley asked politely.

"Chicago," was Keisha's response.

"Do you like Cainsville?" Hartley tried again.

"No," Keisha said curtly.

"I know it's hard being the new kid, but give it a chance. You might like it here," Hartley encouraged.

"I don't want to give it a chance. I hate this stupid little town, and I don't need your help. Got it?" Keisha replied.

"Got it," Hartley simply said as she turned and walked away. That was the last conversation that Hartley and Keisha would have for a while. Hartley watched over the next few weeks as Carmen befriended Keisha. Keisha seemed to blend perfectly into Carmen's group. Keisha even decided to try out for the cheerleading squad.

Homecoming week brought the usual annual craziness and pranks to Cainsville High. Every year the cheerleaders selected one of their fellow students to be the victim of the cheerleaders' prank. This year Carmen, the newly appointed cheerleading captain, chose Hartley as the prank victim. Carmen decided the squad would kidnap Hartley, tie her up, and drop her in a deserted field. They would make her spend the night alone and pick her up in the morning.

Carmen decided to test one of the cheerleader hopefuls. She selected Keisha to be the one to kidnap Hartley. Keisha had an uneasy feeling about it, though. As she watched Hartley, waiting for the right time to kidnap her, she saw what a good person Hartley was. Hartley was always stopping to help someone pick up their books or opening doors for people. She knew Hartley didn't deserve what Carmen had planned for her.

Hartley hadn't given Keisha much thought since their first encounter. It came as a surprise to her when she had a vision of Keisha being killed in a tornado. Hartley saw Keisha bound and lying on the ground in a cornfield when a tornado hit. Hartley had no idea why Keisha was tied up or where she was, but she planned on finding out.

Carmen was upset when Keisha failed to kidnap Hartley. She took her anger out by making Keisha the new kidnap victim. She told her fellow cheerleaders the plan in the girl's bathroom. They would kidnap Keisha that night and leave her in the Miller's cornfield. The Millers were on vacation and no one would know Keisha was out there. Hartley happened to be in a bathroom stall when she heard Carmen's plan. Hartley made a plan of her own. She would wait for the group of cheerleaders to leave Keisha then rescue her.

Hartley carefully followed Carmen's car to the Miller's farm, a couple miles north outside of Cainsville. She saw the cheerleaders pull Keisha out of the trunk and take her somewhere in the corn field. Hartley waited for them to disappear in the corn stalks before she followed them inside.

Hartley heard Keisha crying and begging Carmen not to leave her. Hartley felt sick when she heard Carmen laughing. How could anyone be so cruel? In the distance, Hartley heard the distinct sound of thunder. Did Carmen have any idea what the weather was going to be like? Surely she wouldn't leave someone out here, knowing they could get seriously hurt. Hartley tried to shake the thought from her head, but deep down she had a sick feeling the answer was yes.

As she watched the group of girls leave and heard their car drive away, Hartley emerged from the corn. Keisha had stopped screaming for help and was crying to herself. Rain began falling from the sky, and Hartley knew they didn't have much time.

"Keisha!" Hartley yelled out as she ran toward her.

"Hartley!" Keisha cried out in disbelief.

Hartley began untying the ropes that bound Keisha's legs and arms. "Keisha, there's a tornado coming. We have to get out of here right now, okay?" Keisha nodded in reply.

By that time, the rain was pouring down and lightning was flashing across the sky. Hartley knew the Millers had a storm cellar, the only problem was finding it. The corn was so thick and the rain was pouring down making it difficult to see anything. Hartley felt Keisha holding on to her shoulder as Hartley guided their way through the field. She finally saw the house and the cellar and not a moment too soon. The tornado from Hartley's vision descended from the sky and was making its way toward them.

As Hartley and Keisha locked the cellar door, they heard the screaming winds of the twister. They sat across from each other on the cement floor of the cellar and waited for the storm to pass. The only light came through the cracks in the cellar door, barely illuminating the small space. Hartley looked at Keisha to see she was still crying.

"Keisha we're going to be alright. The storm will pass in a few minutes. Tornadoes happen here all the time." Hartley tried to say something calming.

"She was going to leave me out there to die. What type of person does that?" Keisha asked as she sobbed harder.

"It was just a stupid prank. I'm sure they didn't know how bad the weather was going to be." Hartley tried to convince Keisha, but the truth was she couldn't even convince herself.

"How did you know where to find me?" Keisha asked as her crying was easing up.

"I heard Carmen talking about it in the bathroom," Hartley said. It was the truth. Not the whole truth, but part of the truth.

"You came to help me. Why? I was so mean to you," Keisha asked.

Hartley sighed and replied, "Because no one deserves to be treated like that, no matter how mean they are."

"Thank you," Keisha said quietly.

"Don't mention it," Hartley said simply.

Keisha was in awe of Hartley. Hartley had risked her own life to save Keisha. At that moment

Keisha realized Hartley was the most kindhearted human being she had ever met. She knew she would be forever indebted to Hartley for saving her life.

From that day on, Hartley had a best friend. At first Hartley wasn't sure if Keisha was trying to repay her for saving her life or if she really wanted to be friends. As time progressed, Hartley realized that Keisha was a true friend.

* * * * * * * * * * * * * * * * * *

When Keisha slammed Hartley's locker, the sound brought Hartley back to the present interrupting Hartley's thoughts.

"News travels fast" Keisha said, "and when Hartley Redfield gets in trouble, that is news."

"I fell asleep during Mr. Mercer's class and he flipped out," Hartley answered her friend.

"Okay, Sleeping Beauty, let me help you to class while you give me the details," Keisha said taking Hartley's arm and guiding her down the hall to Spanish class.

"So, why were you talking to Tyler?" Keisha asked, searching for some new gossip.

"I have to tutor him as a part of Mr. Mercer's punishment," Hartley said. She was still clutching her forehead.

"Some punishment. I bet you don't mind that at all. Getting to cozy up with Tyler and help him 'study'," Keisha said putting air quotes around the word study.

"Don't start, Keisha. I already have a headache," Hartley groaned. "Besides, he has a girlfriend, or did you forget?"

"Come on, Hartley, they're not married. You know he has a thing for you. Give him a push. Ask him to prom," Keisha said excitedly.

Prom was a few weeks away and everyone was in a last minute panic for a date. Since Mike Carter asked Keisha last week, she had made it her personal mission to find Hartley a date. The truth was that Hartley seriously doubted anyone would ask her. No one had the year before, and she was not about to ask anyone. Prom was not a big deal to her, but to the rest of the school it was a very big deal. At the moment Hartley was more concerned about the vision of a tornado trying to kill her than finding a prom date.

"He is going with his girlfriend. I don't even want to go to prom," Hartley sighed. However, Keisha was not convinced.

"Well, I've been asking around and there are a couple of ninth graders still available. You could ask one of them. I'm sure they would love to go with you," Keisha said.

"I'm not that desperate, but thanks anyway," Hartley answered.

"You have to go, Hartley, it's our senior year," begged Keisha.

"All I care about is graduation and getting out of this town," Hartley said firmly.

Hartley had been waiting to hear back from Stanford University, her dream college. She couldn't wait to trade Kansas and tornadoes in for California and sunshine. Deep down, Hartley knew she only wanted to go to Stanford because her parents went there. She had applied to other schools, including the University of Oklahoma, only as back-ups. Her heart was set on Stanford and becoming a doctor. She had applied for early admissions on all her applications, and as it was early May, she should be hearing back from them any day now.

"Whatever, I know you want to go to prom, everyone does," replied Keisha as they arrived at Hartley's Spanish class.

Hartley rolled her eyes and told her friend, "I'll see you at lunch."

Spanish was far less eventful than Calculus, which Hartley was very grateful for. In British literature, Mrs. Shelby gave back their essays on Macbeth; Hartley received an A. English was easy for Hartley and had always been one of her favorite classes. Her next class was government which passed slowly. Hartley tried hard to focus on the lecture about the legislative branch but found it was very difficult. She was doodling squiggles that kept turning into tornadoes in the margins of her notes.

As she gazed around the class, she realized that Carmen was glaring at her. Hartley interpreted the scowls as a sign that Carmen was unhappy that Hartley would be tutoring her boyfriend. Hartley, who was accustomed to Carmen's glares, managed to ignore her.

Hartley was relieved when the bell rang for lunch. She was halfway through the day. Hartley joined Keisha in the hallway and together they made their way to the lunchroom. Hartley waited for Keisha to get her lunch, and then they headed toward the far corner of the lunch room where their table was situated. Unfortunately, they had to pass the table in the middle of the lunchroom where all the popular kids sat, including Carmen.

Hartley knew Carmen would be waiting with her usual animosity. Sure enough, as she passed the table she heard Carmen call out to her. "Nice outfit, Hartley, where did you get it? Been shopping at the local dumpster, again?" Carmen asked harshly. Hartley heard the table full of Carmen's friends shriek with laughter.

Hartley turned to face Carmen and said, "Yeah, I did. I can't afford to shop at Clothes for Hoes like you," and walked away. Keisha laughed the whole way to their table. Hartley was rather shocked she had been able to think of a comeback so quickly. Usually she just ignored Carmen and kept walking. This day was definitely turning out to be strange.

"Nice one, Hartley, did you see the look on her face? Priceless." Keisha said, giddy with joy.

"I miss the days when she used to pretend I was invisible," sighed Hartley.

"Ignore her, Hartley; she's just jealous of you," Keisha explained.

"Jealous of me? What do I have that she wants? Cows? Chores? My real nose?" Hartley asked. Surely Keisha was joking with her. There was no way Carmen could ever be jealous of Hartley. Carmen had everything.

"You're naturally pretty, nice, and the smartest girl in school. Of course Carmen is jealous, and she knows Tyler is secretly in love with you," said Keisha in a matter of fact tone.

"Thank you, Keisha, but you couldn't be more wrong. Tyler is not in love with me. He's not even friends with me," Hartley replied.

"If you ask me, I think Tyler is ready for an upgrade," Keisha said.

Hartley just shook her head in disagreement and finished eating her lunch. Keisha continued talking. Hartley was grateful for her friend's ability to carry on a conversation by herself. Hartley had always struggled with making conversation. Keisha had the opposite problem and struggled with not talking. It was one of the reasons why the two were such good friends.

Chapter 4

The bell rang signaling the end of lunch. Hartley parted with Keisha and headed to her next class, Advanced Biology. Advanced Biology was Hartley's second favorite class. She knew she favored English and Science because they had been her parent's favorite subjects. Hartley also liked the class because of her teacher, Mr. Pooler. He was Hartley's favorite teacher, not only because of the subject he taught, but because he was kind and fair.

All of the other teachers at Cainsville High were afraid to discipline Carmen due to the fact she was the Mayor's (and head of the school board) daughter. If Carmen insulted Hartley in front of a teacher, they would just pretend they didn't hear it. If Carmen insulted Hartley in front of Mr. Pooler, she would get detention. After this occurred a couple times, Carmen learned to keep her mouth shut.

James Pooler was older, in his sixties. He wasn't very tall and had a bald spot on the top of his head. The few patches of hair he had left were turning from blond to gray. He wore glasses which seemed to enlarge his eyes. He always dressed in brightly colored Hawaiian shirts which reminded

Hartley of someone going to a Jimmy Buffett concert, rather than a high school science teacher.

Hartley sat down at her lab station at the front of the class. Two people sat at each station. Since there was an odd number, Hartley sat by herself. She didn't mind. She usually finished her work first, and Mr. Pooler let her help the other students. Carmen sat with Tyler at the lab station next to Hartley. The bell rang, and Mr. Pooler began the lesson for the day.

"Okay, class, this week we will be studying the atmosphere and the weather," Mr. Pooler said. "And I thought since we live in the heart of Tornado Alley, we would start off with tornadoes."

"Oh no," Hartley mentally groaned. *"Just what I need, another reminder."*

"Let's see what you already know about tornadoes. Can anybody tell me, in scientific terms, what a tornado is?" Mr. Pooler asked. "Anybody? How about you, Carmen?"

Carmen clearly did not know how to explain scientifically what a tornado was. Not wanting to look stupid in front of the class, she quickly diverted the attention to Hartley.

"No, Mr. Pooler, I don't know, but why don't you ask Hartley? She's had personal experience with a tornado," Carmen said scornfully as she looked at Hartley.

Hartley's pulse began to race, and she thought she might be sick. How could Carmen possibly know that she had visions of tornadoes? Hartley had never slipped up. Carmen couldn't know. Then Hartley realized what the comment really meant. Carmen was making fun of how Hartley's parents had died. She was the only person in the class to lose parents in a tornado. She couldn't believe one person could be so cruel.

Mr. Pooler misinterpreted the panicked look on Hartley's face to mean that she was upset. He quickly sprang into action. "Why, thank you for the suggestion, Carmen. That is a wonderful idea."

Hartley looked at Mr. Pooler as if he had just lost his mind. Mr. Pooler winked at Hartley, telling her that he had a plan. "Class, I'm going to ask Hartley a series of questions. If she gets all of them right, then I won't give any homework, quizzes, or tests this week." The class eagerly agreed to this arrangement although Hartley was still felling like she might be sick.

"First question, Hartley, what is a tornado?" Mr. Pooler began.

Hartley, of course, knew the answer. Since she discovered her special ability, she had researched everything there was to know about tornadoes. She was practically a walking science book that could quote tornado facts.

She took a deep breath and answered the question. "A tornado is a violently rotating column of air that is in contact with the ground and extends downward from a cumuliform cloud and often, but not always, is visible as a funnel cloud."

"Very good, Hartley. Now can you please tell us how tornadoes form?" Mr. Pooler asked.

"Tornadoes usually form from thunderstorms. When warm moist air from the Gulf of Mexico combines with cool dry air from Canada, the two air masses create instability in the atmosphere. A change in wind direction and an increase in wind speed with increasing height create a horizontal spinning effect in the lower atmosphere. Rising air within the updraft tilts the rotating air vertically, forming a tornado."

"What is a dryline?" Mr. Pooler continued grilling Hartley with questions, certain that she already knew the answers to all of them.

"A dryline is a boundary between masses of humid air and dry air, which is often the site for development of thunderstorms," Hartley explained.

"Please tell the class the difference between a tornado watch and a tornado warming," Mr. Pooler went on to ask.

"A tornado watch means that the conditions are right for a tornado to form. A tornado warning is when a tornado has been spotted on the ground," Hartley replied.

"Okay, I think you've had enough questions - unless you want to go double or nothing?" Mr. Pooler asked the class.

"Do you mean we would get two weeks of no homework if Hartley got the question right?" Chesney asked from the back of the class.

"No, actually I would not assign anymore homework for the rest of the year," Mr. Pooler said.

Hartley's classmates were amazed by her knowledge and had complete confidence in her ability to answer the question correctly. They shouted in agreement and cheered her on. Hartley, on the other hand, was less confident in her abilities.

"Okay, Hartley, I need you to calculate the wind speed of a tornado that has traveled over a span of seventy five miles in less than eighteen minutes," Mr. Pooler asked.

"I can't," Hartley replied processing the question. The class groaned in disappointment behind her.

"That's too bad," Mr. Pooler said.

"No, I mean I can't calculate that because the wind speed is determined by the Fujita scale which rates the strength of the tornado by the amount of damage the tornado causes," Hartley explained.

Mr. Pooler broke into a smile. "Class, you can thank Hartley for not having any homework for the rest of the year." Most of the class erupted into praise for Hartley although she heard a few people say "nerd" under their breath.

Mr. Pooler began lecturing, making sure to avoid asking anymore questions. The bell rang and the class began to leave. As Hartley headed toward the door she heard Mr. Pooler say, "I'd like a word, Hartley".

"That was some very impressive work you did today, Hartley," Mr. Pooler told her.

"Thanks," replied Hartley.

"Have you heard back from any colleges yet?" Mr. Pooler asked.

"Not yet, but I did early admissions, so it should be any day now," Hartley said.

"Did you happen to apply to the University of Oklahoma?" Mr. Pooler asked.

"Yes, but only as a backup," Hartley informed him.

"I know you want to go to Stanford, but a friend of mine who teaches Atmospheric Science at Oklahoma sent me this scholarship form to give to the student who has the highest GPA in my class." Mr. Pooler said handing her a packet of papers.

"Thanks, Mr. Pooler, but shouldn't you give this to the person who actually wants to be a meteorologist?" Hartley asked.

"Hartley, you are the only student who has an A average, and half the kids in your class aren't even going to college. I think you're the only one who has a shot at this," Mr. Pooler told her.

Hartley was still unconvinced. Considering her relationship with weather, becoming a meteorologist was the last thing she wanted to do. Still, she didn't want to be rude, so she took the papers.

Mr. Pooler sensed her hesitation. "I know you're going to get into Stanford and become a doctor, but this is a good back up in case things don't work out the way you plan. This scholarship is a full ride. Just fill it out. Even if you get it, you don't have to accept it."

Hartley smiled. She knew she didn't have the money to pay for Stanford, let alone medical school. The little money she had from her parents wouldn't cover everything. She had applied for every scholarship she could find, so why not try this one?

"Okay, I'll give it a try. Thanks, Mr. Pooler," Hartley said as she left the room.

While the rest of the seniors had to take World History, Hartley spent the next period as the office assistant. Hartley had applied to take classes early and had finished her history requirements last year. The school secretary, Mrs. Phillips, was very happy to have Hartley as an assistant. She allowed Hartley to do everything from filling out official school forms to running errands for the principal.

Hartley didn't mind at all. It was convenient when she needed to access the tornado alarm whenever she had one of her visions.

It was a slow day in the office, so when Hartley arrived, Mrs. Phillips and Principal Burns decided to take a late lunch and leave Hartley in charge. She had the elderly school nurse, Mrs. Welter, as company. Mrs. Welter rarely had any patients, so she usually took a two hour nap every afternoon. Hartley didn't mind. She preferred being alone to being in a class full of students.

As Mrs. Welter's snores filled the office, Hartley started working on the homework Mr. Mercer assigned. She used the school copier to copy her notes for Tyler to use. She couldn't help but worry that she might end up with detention for the rest of the year and what that would do to her permanent record. She hoped that Tyler wasn't having too much trouble and that her job as a tutor would be easy.

As Hartley worked, she tried to concentrate on her homework, but her thoughts kept drifting to the horrible sight of the tornado she had seen in her vision. Normally, Hartley didn't fret over a vision. She usually just came up with a plan to help whomever the vision involved, but this was something entirely different. She had never failed to finish a vision. Neither had she ever had a vision that included herself, nor had she ever failed to know who was with her. Typically she had no reason to be afraid, but with this vision she did.

To ease her mind, she checked the copy of the *Cainsville Gazette* that Mrs. Phillips always had on her desk. As she searched for clues in the weekly forecast, she found nothing. The forecast only predicted bright sunny weather for the week. Hartley was puzzled, and for the first time in her life, she hoped to have another vision to fill in the details.

Chapter 5

The bell finally rang to end the school day, and Hartley headed home remembering she had to help Uncle Wyatt fix a tractor. Uncle Wyatt had started teaching Hartley from a young age how to manage a farm and how to repair everything on it. She knew what to feed the cows, chickens, pigs, and horses. She knew how to drive every tractor. She knew how to plant corn and wheat and how to pick them. Hartley knew most eighteen-year-old girls didn't have the farm skills she had. She also knew that her aunt and uncle relied on her to help keep the farm going.

Hartley pulled into the long, dirt driveway that led to the old farmhouse on top of the hill. The once-white paint that covered the house had faded to a soft ivory color. The tin roof had faded as well. Hartley loved to hear the sound of rain falling against it, almost as much as she loved to sit in the swing on the wrap-around porch and read. There was an American flag hanging from the front porch. The house itself was surrounded by brightly colored flowers that were in full bloom. They had been planted by Aunt Laura in an effort to make the house look less shabby. Hartley didn't care how faded or old the house was. It was her home.

As she parked the truck, she noticed Bob Dylan was waiting patiently for her on the steps. Hartley loved that he did this every day. She could always count on her dog to make her day better. As she walked up the steps, Bob Dylan greeted her with a bark and wagging tail. Hartley returned the greeting by patting him on the head.

As Hartley walked through the front door, the warm aroma of baked goods surrounded her. She found a fresh plate of chocolate-chip cookies waiting for her on the counter. Aunt Laura was an excellent cook and enjoyed trying to make Hartley fat. She grabbed a cookie and went in the living room where she found her aunt working at her sewing table.

Besides her amazing baking skills, Aunt Laura was an incredible seamstress. She could mend any garment and fix any seam. She was the town's official seamstress. People would bring their clothes to Aunt Laura to be taken up, taken in, let out, or patched up. It was not unusual to find her fixing someone else's clothes. She also designed clothes. Half of Hartley's closet consisted of Aunt Laura's original creations.

As Hartley watched her aunt working, she thought of how pretty she was. Aunt Laura didn't look like the rest of the moms around Cainsville. She had a head full of vibrant red hair that she usually wore piled on top of her head. She had a splattering of freckles across her face which accented her clear blue eyes. Aunt Laura didn't dress like other moms, either. Her wardrobe consisted of tight jeans, colorful tops, and original designs she made herself.

When Aunt Laura saw Hartley enter the room, she quickly hid whatever she was working on. Hartley gave her a baffled look. Her aunt was normally very open about everything with Hartley; sometimes she was a little too open. Before Hartley could ask what she was working on, Aunt Laura started the conversation.

"Hi, sweetheart, how was your day?" asked Aunt Laura, who was smiling a little too hard at Hartley.

"Long," replied Hartley.

"Well, at least you're home now. Wyatt's waiting on you outside to help him," said Aunt Laura still smiling. Hartley had the strange suspicion that her aunt wanted her out of the room.

"Okay, I'm going to go change," Hartley said as she began to climb the stairs. She stopped midway and told her aunt, "I might be late for dinner. I have to help Tyler with our math homework." Hartley left the details of why she had to help Tyler for later.

"That's fine, we'll wait for you," Aunt Laura said.

"Alright," Hartley said as she headed upstairs to change. Her aunt did not usually act so strange, but Hartley just added it as another aspect of her peculiar day.

Hartley went upstairs and changed into a pair of old jeans and a t-shirt because she knew she would likely be covered in dirt and grease. She headed outside to find Uncle Wyatt. She found him, or rather, his feet sticking out from underneath the tractor.

"Uncle Wyatt?" Hartley asked as she kicked the tip of his boot. It was not uncommon for Uncle Wyatt to catch up on his sleep while pretending to work on something.

"Hey, kid," Uncle Wyatt replied as he rolled out from under the tractor, smiling at Hartley.

When Uncle Wyatt smiled, Hartley could understand why her Aunt Laura ran off and married him when she was just eighteen. Uncle Wyatt was tall and had sandy blond hair which was beginning to show signs of thinning. He usually kept it covered with the same scruffy baseball cap he had been wearing for years. His smile could light up a room but was now surrounded by a few laugh lines. Hartley thought both her aunt and uncle had aged well. She began to wonder what her own parents would look like if they had been given the chance to grow old.

"What seems to be the problem?" Hartley asked.

"Engine trouble again, but I think we can manage it," he said. "Grab the tools and give me a hand."

"How was school today?" Uncle Wyatt asked Hartley as they were working.

"Oh, you know the usual. I had another vision, but the teacher woke me up before I could finish, threatening to give me detention unless I can get Tyler to pass Calculus. I was insulted by Carmen, again, and had to show off my mad science skills in Biology," replied Hartley jokingly.

"Is that all?" Uncle Wyatt tried to ask in a serious tone, but Hartley could hear the laughter in his voice.

"Oh yeah – and I think I gave myself a concussion with my locker door," Hartley added.

"So who was the vision about?" Uncle Wyatt asked curiously.

"Me, I think, but there was someone else with me screaming," Hartley said.

"Where were you?" asked Uncle Wyatt.

"I was in my truck driving when I saw the tornado in the rearview mirror. It was the biggest tornado I've ever seen, at least a mile wide. Then I heard someone screaming next to me, but when I turned to see who it was, Mr. Mercer woke me up," Hartley said.

"Was it Laura with you?" Uncle Wyatt asked concerned for the safety of his family.

"No, I don't think so," Hartley replied, also having the same thought, "the screaming was too high pitched to be her voice. I'm not sure who it could be."

"Well, I'm sure you'll figure it out. You always do." Uncle Wyatt said reassuringly.

"I know, but this vision feels different from the others." Hartley said.

"Different how?" Uncle Wyatt asked.

"This vision scared me," Hartley confessed.

"And you've never felt scared by the other ones?" Uncle Wyatt asked. He stopped working and turned to face Hartley.

"Before, I had this feeling that everything would be okay. Deep down, I knew I would figure it out. But this one feels strange. Like something really bad is going to happen and I won't be able to stop it." Hartley said, struggling to explain. "Why can't I just be normal like other kids?" she asked in frustration.

"Look, Hartley, I know this hasn't been any easy thing for you to deal with, running around helping people all the time without them knowing or saying thank you. But - you do an amazing job and I couldn't be more proud of you. You don't need to be afraid. You'll figure this out. Laura and I will do everything to help you. I promise I won't let

anything bad happen to you. Do you understand?"
Uncle Wyatt said.

Hartley shook her head in response. Her
uncle gave her a hug and they got back to work. She
wasn't convinced, though. She knew Uncle Wyatt
and Aunt Laura would help her; they always did. It
was the feeling of uncertainty in the pit of her
stomach that was troubling her. All she could do
was pray she found an answer before the tornado
hit.

They finally got the tractor working late in
the afternoon. Hartley rushed to shower and get
ready for her tutoring session. She grabbed her
Calculus book and notes and started walking across
the field that separated the two farms.

Hartley climbed the steps of the Heath's
porch at exactly five o'clock. Hartley prided herself
on her punctuality. She checked in the driveway for
Tyler's car before knocking on the door. His red
1965 Mustang sat proudly in the driveway. Hartley
knew how much Tyler loved his car. Tyler had
spent the entire summer restoring it with his father
before he died.

Theodore Heath passed away suddenly last
year of a heart attack. His death had left Cainsville
in shock and disbelief. He had seemed perfectly
healthy. Hartley had always liked Mr. Heath. He
was a kind and hardworking man. His passing was
especially hard on the family. Hartley and her

family did everything they could to help. Hartley and Aunt Laura babysat the twins for free, and Uncle Wyatt offered to help Tyler with their farm while Mrs. Heath found a job.

Hartley knocked on the door, and it was answered by Mrs. Heath. Dianne Heath was a nice-looking woman of thirty eight who had light brown hair and green eyes. In the past she always had a smile on her face, but nowadays she looked tired. Hartley knew her husband's death had been hard on her, but Mrs. Heath still managed to be the sweet women she had grown up knowing.

"Hartley! Good to see you, come in, come in," she said ushering Hartley into the house.

"Hi, Mrs. Heath, I was looking for Tyler. We're supposed to study together" Hartley told her, not wanting to embarrass Tyler by saying 'tutor'.

"He's not back from practice yet, but he should be home any minute. Come in and wait for him," she said. Hartley thought that was odd since his car was in the driveway. She then realized that Carmen had probably driven him to practice. Hartley followed Mrs. Heath into the kitchen where they found the twins having a tea party.

Maddie and Mollie were six-year-old identical twins. They looked just like their older brother, except they were little girls. It was extremely difficult to tell them apart, but Hartley knew the trick. Maddie always wore pink and

Mollie always wore blue. Being their babysitter, Hartley had grown close to the adorable pair. At the sight of Hartley, the two started shouting with joy.

"Hartley, Hartley!" They cried simultaneously.

"Hey!" she returned the greeting with the same enthusiasm.

"Hartley, have a tea party with us," the twins begged her.

"Girls, don't bother Hartley. She came here to study with Tyler." Mrs. Heath told her girls.

"No, it's okay. I love tea parties," Hartley said, reassuring the twins after seeing their disappointed faces.

Mrs. Heath smiled in gratitude. "You two behave while I do laundry," Mrs. Heath said as she left the room.

"Hartley, sit with us," the twins pleaded. They were sitting at their small kid's table. Hartley scrunched down and balanced herself on one of the tiny chairs. The other chair was occupied by a teddy bear wearing a hat.

"You have to get dressed for the party," the twins told her. Hartley noticed that Maddie was wearing a pink tutu and pearls, and Mollie was wearing a blue tutu and oversized sunglasses.

"Sorry, I didn't know." Hartley apologized for the jeans and t-shirt which were obviously not the appropriate attire for a tea party.

"You can wear some of our stuff," Maddie said, dashing from the room. She returned a moment later with a pink crown and a blue boa.

"Thanks," Hartley said donning the crown and boa.

"You look pretty," Mollie said.

"Thank you. You both look beautiful," Hartley replied.

They poured the tea which was actually water and snacked on the fresh-baked brownies. While taking a sip of her "tea", Hartley was surprised by the question Maddie asked.

"Hartley, why can't you be Tyler's girlfriend?"

Hartley nearly choked on her tea, and ended up spitting it all over herself. She replied, "Because he already has a girlfriend. Carmen is his girlfriend."

"We don't like her!" shouted Maddie.

"She's mean!" said Mollie mimicking Maddie's tone.

"I know she is, but Tyler likes her, so you should try too." Hartley tried to reason, but she had to agree with them.

They were about to begin their rants again, but at that moment they heard the front door opening. A few seconds later Tyler appeared, followed by the subject of their conversation, Carmen.

"What's going on?" Tyler asked, while Carmen hovered behind him.

"We're just hanging out, having a tea party," Hartley replied casually, trying to ignore how ridiculous she must look.

"Of course," Tyler said laughing. "You look better in the boa than I do when they make me play tea party." Tyler said to Hartley, then turned to the twins to ask, "Where's mom?"

"Doing laundry," they said simultaneously. Hartley wondered if all twins could answer in unison and began to speculate whether her aunt and mom did the same thing when they were young.

Hartley noticed the twins were returning the scowls that Carmen was giving Hartley. Tyler turned to Carmen and said, "Thanks for the ride". He kissed her on the cheek and then left the room to find his mom.

Carmen waited for Tyler to leave the room before insulting Hartley. She always seemed to wait for Tyler to be out of earshot before insulting her.

"Nice crown, Hartley. It's a shame it's the closest you'll ever come to being prom queen," she said viciously.

Before Hartley could respond, the twins had launched themselves at Carmen. Hartley had to grab them by the tutus to keep them from pouncing on her.

Carmen, shocked by their outburst, took a step back. When she regained her composure, she said, "At least you have some friends, Hartley," and left. Hartley considered turning the twins loose on her, but decided against it. She only released them when she heard the front door slam.

By that time, Mrs. Heath and Tyler returned. Mrs. Heath took the girls outside to play so Hartley and Tyler could study. They started working after Hartley took off her tea party attire.

Three hours later, Hartley was exhausted. It was going to be more difficult that Hartley had anticipated. Tyler hadn't been exaggerating when he said he was bad. He was beginning to understand the concept, but they had many hours of work ahead of them.

Hartley started walking toward the door and was surprised when Tyler grabbed her books and followed her outside.

"I'm pretty sure I know the way home," Hartley said laughing.

"You just spent the last three hours trying to explain calculus to me. The least I can do is walk you home," he said.

Hartley didn't bother arguing; she didn't mind the company. It reminded her of when they were younger. Every time Hartley spent the day at Tyler's house he would always walk her home. She felt a twinge of sadness. She missed the old days when she was friends with Tyler.

They walked in silence for a little while. It wasn't an awkward silence for Hartley, like it was with most people. Tyler started the conversation by asking, "Have you heard back from any colleges yet?"

"No, not yet, but it should be any day now," Hartley said. "How's your scholarship coming? Everything good to go?" Hartley knew Tyler was getting a full ride from the University of Oklahoma.

"Yeah, I sign next week," Tyler said wearily.

"Aren't you excited?" Hartley asked. She knew the only thing Tyler ever wanted to do was play baseball, but he didn't sound too thrilled at the prospect of playing college baseball.

"Yeah, it's great. I guess I'm just a little, I mean I'm..." Tyler struggled.

"You're just a little nervous about going to college and starting over in a new place." Hartley finished his sentence for him.

"Yes," Tyler confessed.

"It's okay to be nervous about college, everyone is," Hartley said reassuringly.

"You're not. You can't wait to run away to California," Tyler said.

"Can you blame me? High school hasn't been that great for me," Hartley replied.

"What are you talking about? High school was great," Tyler said.

"Yeah, for you. You're popular. You're the star of the baseball team. You date the most popular girl in school. You have a cool car. Everyone likes you. I'm not popular or athletic. I don't have a boyfriend. I'm invisible to half the school and the other half hates me because I'm smart. I have a truck that belongs in the Smithsonian. I only have two friends and one of them is a golden retriever. High school sucks. College can only get better," Hartley finished her speech.

They walked in a silence a few minutes until Tyler said, "We're friends."

"No, no we're not," Hartley laughed.

"What?" Tyler replied with a shocked expression on his face.

"We are not friends." Hartley said firmly.

"How can you say that?" Tyler asked as though Hartley had genuinely hurt his feelings.

"When was the last time we spent any time together without being forced by a teacher? When was the last time we sat together at lunch? When was the last time we had a conversation other than, 'Hey, how's it going'?" Hartley asked.

Tyler didn't answer, and Hartley knew she had made her point. Tyler thought about what Hartley had said. Had it really been that long since they hung out together? They used to sit together at lunch every day. They used to spend hours talking to each other about everything. When did that end? Hartley had been his closest friend. When had that changed?

When they reached Hartley's house, Tyler handed her books to her and thanked her for her help. Before turning around to walk home Tyler called out to Hartley.

"I'm going to prove to you that we're still friends, Hartley Redfield."

Hartley just smiled at him. She doubted that he could, but she hoped that Tyler would prove her wrong.

Chapter 6

The next day turned out to be better than the previous. Calculus was a quiet event. Mr. Mercer seemed satisfied with Tyler's progress when he answered a question correctly. Hartley assumed she was safe from detention for now. She happily noted that Carmen was absent. It was not unusual for Carmen to skip school on a regular basis.

Today the rumor was that Carmen had skipped school to go prom dress shopping in the city. Hartley cherished the peaceful days when Carmen didn't grace them with her presence. The rest of Hartley's classes passed quickly enough. By lunch Hartley was in a cheerful mood, and she joined Keisha at their table.

"Can I stay at your house Thursday night? My mom has to work nightshift again," Keisha asked. Keisha's mom was an ER nurse at the hospital and occasionally had to work at night. When this happened, Keisha stayed with the Sawyers.

"Sure," Hartley replied. She didn't mind, and Keisha always proved to be entertaining.

"I told my mom that I'm old enough to stay home alone, but she's convinced I'll set the house on fire or throw some crazy party. Isn't that ridiculous? She has no trust in me. Can you believe that? I can't wait to move out on my own. Graduation can't come fast enough." Keisha blabbered on.

Hartley knew Keisha was planning on moving back to Chicago to live with her grandma and go to college. Her dream was to be a news reporter. Hartley thought that would be a great job seeing how Keisha loved to talk.

Keisha was still chattering about something, Hartley wasn't really paying attention. She did notice when Keisha suddenly stopped talking. Hartley looked up to see Tyler sitting down beside her.

"Hello," Tyler simply told both of them as he started to eat his lunch. They continued to stare at him as though he had lost his mind. Finally, Hartley broke the silence.

"What are you doing?" She asked curiously.

"Eating lunch," Tyler replied with a mouth full of food.

"Yes, I can see that," Hartley said slowly. "I mean why are you eating lunch here?"

Tyler just shrugged. Hartley then realized why he was doing this.

"Oh, I get it. You're trying to prove that we're friends," Hartley said. Tyler gave no response, prompting Hartley to continue, "Well, it's going to take more than one lunch to show we're friends." Tyler rolled his eyes at Hartley, but had every intention of proving to her that they were still friends. Keisha was carefully watching the two as they conversed and determined that her earlier statements were true. Tyler was ready for a girlfriend upgrade.

The bell rang, ending the unusual lunch. Hartley and Tyler said goodbye to Keisha and made their way to Biology class. The class advanced peacefully, not a repeat of the previous day. Mr. Pooler taught the class about hurricanes, thankfully, a subject Hartley was less familiar with.

When the bell rang, she made her way to the office to start her hour as office assistant. Mrs. Phillips and Principal Burns left for lunch, and Mrs. Welter's snores filled the office. Hartley kept busy by filing paperwork and was only interrupted when someone walked into the office.

"Hi Hartley!" Chesney said.

"Hey, Chesney. What are you doing here?" asked Hartley curiously. Chesney was the class clown, notorious for skipping class and pulling pranks. Hartley hoped she was not the target of his latest prank.

"I told the teacher I was sick and needed to see the nurse, but that's not true," Chesney said smiling.

"And she believed that? I figured most teachers have learned not to let you out of their sight," Hartley said.

"I stole some ketchup packets from the lunchroom. I got some tissues and was pretending to blow my nose when I poured the ketchup on the tissue and told her I was having a nosebleed. She hates blood and practically threw me out of the room," Chesney said smiling, clearly proud of the fact that he had outsmarted the teacher.

"That's nice." Hartley said, still concerned about the reason Chesney had used so much effort to see her. "Why exactly did you do this?"

"I need your help. I want to ask Ashley to prom," Chesney said.

"Okay, why do you need my help?" Hartley asked inquisitively. She wasn't friends with Ashley. Ashley was one of Carmen's followers and generally hated Hartley.

"She said I had to find a special way to ask her. I want to operate the camera they use to make the morning announcements and broadcast my proposal all over school," Chesney said excitedly.

Hartley felt uneasy. The camera was in Principal Burn's office. This plan required Chesney breaking into the office, turning on the camera, filming himself, and broadcasting it to the entire school. Chesney was not the smartest cookie in the jar and probably couldn't manage it all on his own.

Hartley was also the only one currently in possession of the key to Principal Burns' office.

"I don't know, Chesney, nobody is supposed to go into Principal Burns' office or make an announcement without permission," Hartley said reluctantly.

"Come on, Hartley, you have to help me. I really want to go to prom with Ashley. Please, please help me," Chesney begged giving Hartley's his biggest puppy dog eyes.

Hartley refused to get in trouble for Chesney, but she wanted to help him out.

"Look Chesney, I can't help you," Hartley said firmly. Chesney looked extremely disappointed. "But," Hartley leaned across the desk and began to whisper, "I could accidently leave the key to the office lying here while I go to the supply closet on the other side of the school to look for more toner for the copier. I could also accidently mention that the green button turns on the camera and to broadcast to the whole school you have be to on channel 3. I could also accidentally tell you that Principal Burns and Mrs. Phillips get back at 2:45 sharp, so you only have ten minutes to get all this done," Hartley told Chesney.

"Thank you, Hartley, you're the best!" Chesney said hugging her. Hartley pushed him away and said, "Remember, you heard nothing from me."

"Right! I heard nothing from you." Chesney said winking at her.

Hartley left the office on her fake mission to find toner. She was completely aware that there was no toner in the supply closet on the other side of the school, but she thought she had to give Chesney a chance. She was halfway to the supply closet when she saw Chesney appear on the TV screen at the end of the hallway and stopped to watch.

"Pardon the interruption, but I have a very special announcement to make," Chesney said. He was sitting behind Principal Burn's desk. "I would like to take the time to ask a very special lady a very special question." Chesney was now standing on top of the desk. "Ashley, will you…" Chesney began to say but then ripped of his shirt. He had written the words "GO TO PROM WITH ME?" across his chest in a giant heart.

Laughter could be heard filling all the classrooms. Chesney was still on the screen, but was now wearing a horrified expression. Apparently Principal Burns had returned early from lunch and was now screaming at Chesney. Chesney jumped off the desk and began running around the room, as he was being chased by Principal Burns. There was roaring laughter coming from all the rooms now.

Hartley quickly made her way to the supply closet. She found no toner just as she expected, but grabbed a pack of paper clips and some paper to prove her story of why she was not in the office to Principal Burns and Mrs. Phillips.

When she arrived back into the office she found that Principal Burns was still yelling at Chesney. Mrs. Welter had even woken up to witness the excitement. Hartley took her place behind the desk next to Mrs. Phillips who was trying not to pretend she was not watching the scene.

"Hartley, you missed all the excitement," Mrs. Phillips told her. Hartley knew Mrs. Phillips lived to gossip and was eager to share the story.

"What happened? I was getting stuff from the supply closet," Hartley said innocently.

"Why, Chesney broke into Principal Burns' office and was broadcasting himself to the whole school," Mrs. Phillips said scandalized.

"No! He must have broken in while I was gone," Hartley said, covering her tracks.

"Oh, I know you wouldn't let anything like that happen, Hartley," Mrs. Phillips said comfortingly. "Some students are just so wild."

In the end, Chesney ended up with two weeks' detention. Ashley apparently thought Chesney's proposal was special enough because she agreed to go to prom with him. Prom fever seemed to be spreading through the school, and Hartley was the only one who was immune.

Students were taking prom extremely seriously, because the proposals were getting more outrageous. Cars were covered in post-its spelling out 'Prom?'and giant balloon bouquets were being delivered daily, poems and songs were being written and performed.

Hartley, however, had more important things to worry about. She was still trying to figure out when her vision was going to take place. The thought was always in the back of her mind, nagging her constantly. Hartley wished that she knew when the tornado was going to hit, but she was just going to have to wait.

Chapter 7

Later that afternoon, Tyler was walking Hartley home after their second tutoring session. Their conversation turned to the prom frenzy that had taken over the entire school.

"That was a nice thing you did for Chesney," Tyler said.

"I don't know what you're talking about."

"Really? Because the Chesney I know has trouble tying his shoe laces, much less breaking into the office and working a video camera all by himself," Tyler said.

"I didn't have anything to do with that," Hartley replied with a smile. Tyler just gave her a look which seemed to say 'I know you're lying'.

"Maybe I helped a little," Hartley admitted. "I had to give him a chance."

"So what lucky guy is taking you to prom?" asked Tyler. He found that he was very curious to know.

"No one. I'm not going," Hartley said adamantly.

"Come on, Hartley, you have to go to prom," Tyler said.

"No, I don't," Hartley said, quickly changing the subject. "So how did you ask Carmen to the prom?"

"I didn't," Tyler said.

"But she already told everyone you're going together."

"She never gave me a chance to ask her. She just kind of told me we were going together," Tyler admitted.

"Well, how would you have asked her? Post-its? Balloon bouquet? Skywriting?" Hartley teased.

"No, I'd play it cool," Tyler said. "I would get her alone, no crowds," Tyler started to say.

"So you wouldn't be embarrassed when she refused to go with you?" Hartley joked.

Tyler rolled his eyes at Hartley and continued. "I would buy her favorite flowers and then I would, you know, just ask her, 'Will you go to prom with me?'"

Hartley was pretending to cry.

"What are you doing?" Tyler asked.

"I never knew how romantic you were, Tyler," Hartley laughing as she fake cried.

"I should have never told you," Tyler said as he pretended to storm off.

"I was kidding!" Hartley said as she grabbed his arm, pulling him back.

"Really?" Tyler asked seriously.

"Yes, it sounded very nice. I'm sure Carmen would have loved it," Hartley said sincerely.

As Tyler was describing the scene, he was surprised to find Carmen wasn't the one he was picturing. Instead, the girl standing right in front of him was the one he had been asking to prom, the one who threw her arms around him and kissed him in his daydream. Tyler could feel his face growing hotter.

"Are you okay?" Hartley asked, snapping him back to reality.

"Yeah," Tyler said coolly.

"You know, I'm kind of glad I'm skipping prom," Hartley admitted.

"Why?" Tyler asked. "It's not that bad."

"I just think about how all the girls get to go dress shopping with their moms; how all their dads will be taking a ton of pictures and threatening their dates. I don't get to do that. I don't get to have any special moments with my parents. It really hits me sometimes," Hartley confessed.

"I know how you feel, Hartley. I wish my dad was here to see me get my baseball scholarship and see me walk across the stage at graduation." Tyler said as he grabbed Hartley's hand. "But you can't let it stop you from getting your special moments." They had stopped walking because they had reached her house. He dropped her hand and started walking back without saying anything else.

Hartley stood there and watched him walk away. She was trying to ignore the tingling sensation in her hand and the racing of her heart.

Wednesday brought another day of school and the return of Carmen. Hartley was not happy about either. Carmen forgot to insult Hartley because all she could talk about was the designer dress on which she spent an outrageous amount of money. *A price that could probably fund a whole semester of tuition at college thought Hartley.* Hartley wished she had the financial security Carmen possessed, but she knew she would just have to hope those scholarships would come through.

Hartley had just finished British Lit and was walking to her locker when she saw a poster advertising prom. She noticed the date at the bottom for the first time. She felt the knot form in her stomach, and she knew what that meant. The tornado in her vision would be arriving the day of prom, which was less than two weeks away.

"This is bad," Hartley said aloud.

"What's bad?" Keisha asked.

Hartley jumped. She hadn't realized anyone was standing behind her.

"Prom. Prom is bad, very bad," stuttered Hartley.

Keisha looked at Hartley suspiciously then her face melted into a concerned smile. "If you're worried about not having a date, I have a cousin that you could go with," Keisha said, trying her best to be helpful.

"No thanks. I just wish prom was over," Hartley said. She had no idea how she was going to deal with a tornado on the biggest day of the school year.

"Fine. I really wish you would change your mind. You could go with me and Mike."

Hartley shook her head and walked away from her friend. Not having a date was bad enough, but going as a third wheel was just humiliating. Besides, she had more important things to focus on. She had to figure out exactly where this tornado was planning to hit.

Government passed slowly and finally it was time for lunch. Keisha had to stay late in Spanish to finish a test, so Hartley was on her own. She was going to take advantage of the quietness. She brought a book she had been wanting to read for a while and planned to have a peaceful lunch.

She had already started reading while walking to her table when she was stopped by a chair that flew into her path. She looked over from the table where it came from and was not surprised to see Carmen was the one who had pushed it. Hartley guessed that Carmen was hoping she would trip and break her neck. She was completely shocked when Carmen offered her a seat at her table.

"Why don't you sit with us, Hartley?" Carmen asked. Hartley recognized the fake sweet voice she only used when Tyler or teachers were around.

"No, thank you. I'm fine," Hartley responded politely. There was no way she would be voluntarily sitting at a table with Carmen.

Hartley began to walk away, but the chair was still in her way. Carmen then said, "I insist," Hartley noticed Tyler was also sitting at the table. He nodded to her to tell her it was okay.

Hartley hesitantly took the seat across from Carmen and Tyler. She tried to read but was unfortunately drawn into the conversation.

"So, Hartley, we were just discussing what we're wearing to prom. Have you decided what you're wearing yet?" Carmen asked.

"I'm not going to prom." Hartley answered reluctantly, although she knew Carmen was aware she was not going to prom.

"Why not? It's going to be so much fun," Carmen asked as though she were genuinely concerned that Hartley was going to be missing the prom.

"Prom's not really my thing," Hartley replied.

"I hate that you're not going. Is it because you can't afford a dress? If that's the reason, I'm sure I have something old in my closet that you can borrow. Or are you not going because you don't have a date? Sorry, but I don't think I have any old boyfriends that you can borrow," Carmen said with a grin. All of her friends at the table started laughing.

Hartley felt sick. She knew sitting at this table was a bad idea and had to leave.

"You know, I don't feel very hungry anymore," Hartley said as she left the lunchroom.

Carmen and her friends were still laughing. Tyler wasn't laughing, though. He was finally realizing the kind of person Carmen was.

"Why did you say that?" Tyler asked Carmen angrily.

"It was a joke. We were just having some fun. What is your problem?" Carmen replied defensively.

"That's your idea of fun? She's really upset," Tyler said.

Carmen just shrugged him off as usual, but Tyler was not finished.

"We're done," Tyler said, standing up.

"That's cute. Sit down," Carmen said through gritted teeth, aware that people were beginning to stare.

"I'm serious. We're through. I mean it this time," Tyler said as he started to walk away.

"You can't break up with me now. What about prom?" Carmen shouted, not caring who was looking now.

"Find someone else. We're finished," Tyler said determinedly as he walked out of the cafeteria.

The room was silent. Everyone appeared to be in shock. They had just witnessed the breakup of the most popular couple in school, and no one knew what to think.

Chapter 8

Her evening tutoring session was difficult for Hartley. She barely said a word to Tyler that wasn't math related. As usual, he walked her home after they were done studying. He also attempted to break the awkward silence.

"I'm sorry about what happened today, Hartley," Tyler said.

"Don't," Hartley warned him.

"Don't what?" Tyler asked.

"Don't defend her," Hartley snapped back.

"I'm not defending her," Tyler said defensively.

"Yes, you are. You always do. You always take her side, whether you know it or not."

"I do not," Tyler said.

"I don't even understand why you're with her. I know she's hot, but I never thought you were that shallow," Hartley said, anger taking over.

"Hey, that's enough," Tyler said. Hartley turned to face Tyler.

"She's not nice. She's not smart, and the one thing that she's good at, I'm pretty sure she's doing with every other guy in school," Hartley continued, ignoring Tyler completely.

"Okay, my turn. Why should I take relationship advice from someone who has never even been in a relationship?" Tyler replied.

Hartley turned and walked away, not wanting Tyler to see her tears. What he said had really hurt, especially because it was true.

"Wait - Hartley, I'm sorry," Tyler called out. He was mad at himself. Hartley was the one person he never wanted to hurt.

Hartley was almost home. She was about to turn around and yell at Tyler some more when it happened.

The field she had been standing in disappeared and she was standing in the middle of the school gym. Decorations were hanging everywhere. Hartley recognized the 'Under the Sea' theme from the poster she saw earlier. The dance floor was packed with couples slow dancing.

Over the loud music, Hartley heard the familiar howling of wind. People were beginning to run when the roof started peeling away. Debris was scattered everywhere, hitting and injuring people. Hartley watched in horror as people were being sucked into the funnel. There were people screaming in pain and crying in fear. Hartley was surrounded by darkness and chaos.

The scene changed. She was standing in what once was downtown Cainsville. The town was in ruins. Cars were overturned, buildings were in

shambles. Hartley saw a few bodies scattered over
the debris. She had a feeling that there was more to
see, but she heard someone calling her name.

"Hartley? Hartley! Wake up Hartley!" She
heard Tyler anxiously calling her name. Her head
was swimming and she was working on opening her
eyes. She then heard Tyler calling to someone for
help.

When Hartley opened her eyes she found
that she was lying on the ground, covered in sweat
and slightly shaking. Tyler was standing above her
looking worried. She heard Uncle Wyatt and Aunt
Laura calling her name. She was able to sit up in
time for the vomiting to start. The images of her
school gym and town covered in the bodies of
people she knew were too much for her to stomach.

Aunt Laura held her hair out of her face
while she finished puking. Uncle Wyatt helped her
slowly to her feet. She was still too wobbly to walk,
so Uncle Wyatt scooped her up in his arms like he
did when she was a little girl and carried her home.
She was still having trouble trying to speak. Her
face was wet and she wasn't sure if it was sweat or
tears.

"What's wrong with her? Is she going to be
alright?" Hartley could hear Tyler asking Aunt
Laura behind them.

"She has low blood sugar. She just needs to
eat something. She'll be fine," Aunt Laura said

smoothly, trying to reassure Tyler. Of course Hartley had heard that lie before when she would mysteriously pass out in front of people.

"Are you sure?" Tyler asked. Hartley could still hear the hesitation in his voice. Poor Tyler, Hartley thought. He had no idea what was really happening.

"I'm sure, Tyler. Thank you for walking her home," Aunt Laura said, politely dismissing Tyler.

Uncle Wyatt set Hartley down on the couch, and Aunt Laura brought her a glass of water. Bob Dylan jumped on the couch to sit with her. They waited patiently before asking her what her vision was about.

When she appeared calmer, Uncle Wyatt asked the question, "What did you see, Hartley?"

Hartley gulped, "Prom. Everyone was in the gym dancing, and then the tornado hit. The roof blew off, and the walls collapsed. People were screaming and bleeding. Some were lying on the floor not moving at all. Others were being sucked straight into the funnel. Then I saw the town. It was completely destroyed. It was terrible, seeing everyone die like that. I can't let that happen. I won't let that happen," Hartley said firmly.

"Everything will be alright, Hartley. We'll figure something out." Aunt Laura said encouragingly, although the look on her face did not match. Hartley could tell they were concerned. She was concerned. She had never had a vision that involved so many people, basically the whole town. The thought alone was giving Hartley a headache.

"I don't feel so good. I'm going to go lie down," Hartley said.

"I'll bring you some food up," Aunt Laura said kissing her forehead.

"Don't worry, Hartley. If all else fails, we can sneak out at night and burn the school down. Then they would have to cancel prom," Uncle Wyatt said.

"Thanks, Uncle Wyatt, but I don't think arson is the answer. I like your enthusiasm though." Hartley smiled weakly at her uncle as she climbed the stairs to her room. She heard the patter of feet behind her and could tell Bob Dylan was following her. He sensed that something was not right and didn't let Hartley out of his sight for the rest of the night.

Hartley relaxed a little when she walked into her room. It was nothing spectacular, but it was hers. Her old, white, iron bed stood in the center of the room. It was covered in a faded red, yellow, and blue patchwork quilt that Aunt Laura had made for her when she was little. Opposite of the bed were two doors. One led to her bathroom and the other to her closet. The walls were covered in a pale yellow color. The only decoration that was on the wall was a brightly colored map. Hartley had marked all the places she had traveled and all the places she wanted to travel.

She had a shabby whitewashed dresser and a matching nightstand beside her bed. On the nightstand there was a reading lamp and picture of Hartley and her parents taken a few months before they died. An old oversized, red-checkered armchair sat in the corner. It was one of Hartley's favorite places to read. She had one large window that overlooked the pasture. Under the window sat her desk where she did her homework. On either side of the desk were bookshelves which housed many of Hartley's books.

There were so many books that they wouldn't all fit on the shelves. Some were stacked in the corners; others were hidden under the bed. Books were the one thing that Hartley hoarded. She had inherited her parents' book collection which she treasured. She loved the idea of reading the same stories that her mom and dad had read.

Most of the books were tattered and threadbare because she read them so much. Her favorite book, *The Wizard of Oz,* was in particularly rough shape. Hartley had fallen in love with the story when she was little. She loved the idea that a tornado could transport a simple farm girl to a magical world. She knew it was a kid's story, but she always read it when she was having a bad day.

Hartley contemplated reading it now, but decided she needed to sleep instead.

Hartley fell asleep immediately, but did not have peaceful dreams. She was being chased by a tornado. No matter how fast she ran, she couldn't escape it. At 4 a.m. she gave up on sleep and decided to work on what was really bothering her. She went to her desk and pulled out a notebook. She began to write down the names of everyone in town and tried to think of ideas of how to keep them safe during the tornado.

Writing down all the names wasn't hard considering how small the town was. Coming up with ideas to save them was the challenging part. She also wondered about her first vision. She knew the two had to be related. Where was she going when everyone else was at prom? Hartley had many things to work out.

The first thing she had to figure out was how to keep all the people at prom safe. Hartley assumed that canceling the prom was not an option at this point, so she needed to know how to handle the situation. Secondly, she had to consider the whole town. She had seen Cainsville being destroyed as well. How was she supposed to keep an entire town safe? Finally, she had to figure out where she was driving to when the tornado hit. It was a giant puzzle, and Hartley was the one who had to figure out how the pieces fit together.

Hartley was extremely tired by the time morning came. She had a few small ideas on how to keep a couple of people safe but needed a much larger plan. She was so tired that she nearly fell asleep while eating her pancakes. Her drowsiness didn't escape the notice of her aunt and uncle.

"Hartley, you're too tired to go to school. Why don't you stay home today and rest?" Uncle Wyatt said.

"I can't miss school. I'll take a nap during my office hour." Hartley yawned as she began to pack her book bag.

"Well, wait a few minutes and I'll make you some coffee," Aunt Laura said.

"I forgot Keisha is staying with us tonight, so no tornado talk. Let's try to pretend that we're normal." Hartley told her aunt and uncle. The last thing she needed was a suspicious best friend.

"Normal like this?" Uncle Wyatt said as he made the silliest looking face Hartley had ever seen.

"Forget it," Hartley said too tired even to laugh at his expression. Aunt Laura handed her a cup of coffee as she walked out of the door. She had a feeling it was going to be a really long day.

Chapter 9

Everyone seemed to be in a bad mood in Calculus class. Carmen looked to be in an exceptionally bad mood. Hartley felt a pang of guilt as she searched the room for Tyler. She had been a little hard on him last night. Not to mention the fact that she had experienced a vision in front of him. Tyler was nowhere to be found. He probably wanted to avoid her. Hartley remembered the baseball team had an away game and that he wouldn't be at school today.

Mr. Mercer ordered everyone to create their own word problems with the equations they had been learning and explained that they would solve them together at the end of class. Hartley quickly scribbled down a word problem then spent the rest of class trying to come up with a plan for prom.

She had an idea that would take care of the elementary and middle school students. She was going to pitch the idea of letting them have their own prom to Principal Burns. The middle school students could use the lunchroom and the elementary could use the music room. Both rooms were both made out of concrete blocks and had no windows which would be safe during a tornado.

Most of the kids lived in trailers or older houses. They would be much safer at school.

She could tell Principal Burns how unfair it was that the little kids didn't get an event. She could tell him how much money they could make selling tickets and how all the parents would love to chaperone. How much money local businesses would make selling dresses and flowers. She was going to talk to him during her office aid hour.

Hartley was snapped out of her planning when Mr. Mercer started calling on people to read their word problems out loud. Most of them were very simple and easy to solve. Then Mr. Mercer decided to call on Carmen, who thought Calculus was beneath her and did not bother to write a problem.

"Well, Miss Guilden, could you kindly think of a problem now?" Mr. Mercer asked her politely. Of course, Carmen got the easy treatment. If Hartley refused to do her work, she would be in detention for the rest of her life.

"Okay. If you take the number of friends Hartley has and divide it by the number of parents she has it should equal zero, which is the same as her family's income." Carmen finished. Hartley just sat with her mouth hanging open. She was in shock and couldn't believe that Carmen had said that. The rest of class was rolling with laughter.

"Alright, that is quite enough from you, Miss Guilden. Let's get back to work." Mr. Mercer said as he called on the next student.

Hartley felt herself raise her hand in the air.

"Yes, Miss Redfield?" Mr. Mercer asked.

"I have a problem I'd like to share," Hartley replied calmly.

"Go ahead then," Mr. Mercer said.

"You start with the square root of one hundred and forty four which is twelve. The same amount of men that could be Carmen's real father. Then you divide by four, which is the same amount of plastic surgeries Carmen has had. That leaves you with three, which is still higher than her I.Q.," Hartley finished defiantly. The whole class remained silent. It was the first time someone had dared to confront Carmen. Carmen looked stunned that Hartley had actually embarrassed her.

"THAT IS ENOUGH!" yelled Mr. Mercer. "Miss Redfield, you will be serving detention this afternoon."

"What? What about Carmen?" shouted Hartley.

"Would you like to make it a week?" asked Mr. Mercer.

"No thank you. One day of injustice is enough," Hartley said sarcastically as Mr. Mercer handed her the detention slip.

Thankfully, the bell rang and Hartley left as fast as she could. She was in a terrible mood. She should have stayed home like Uncle Wyatt said. She had just managed to earn herself detention for the first time in her life. It wasn't going to look good on her permanent record. The rest of her classes passed slowly until it was finally time for lunch. Keisha was practically bouncing out of her seat as Hartley sat down at their table.

"Is it true?" Keisha asked as Hartley sat down.

"Probably. What did you hear?" Hartley asked.

"You and Carmen had a throw down in the in middle of math class and you won," Keisha gloated.

"Yeah, and I'm also the only one who got detention after school," Hartley said.

"Wow! Hartley Redfield in detention, what'll happen next?" Keisha asked.

"I'm glad you're amused. I'm not. This goes on my permanent record. Colleges will see this. I don't even know what started this. I mean, I know Carmen is awful, but this is a new degree of hatefulness," Hartley complained.

"Come on, Hartley, you know what started this," Keisha said giving Hartley a reproachful look.

"What are you talking about?" Hartley said. She hadn't done anything out of the ordinary to Carmen, so she wondered what had changed.

"I'm talking about Tyler dumping Carmen in front of the whole school yesterday because she was mean to you," Keisha informed Hartley.

"But…" Hartley stammered. She didn't know anything about it. She had left the lunchroom early after Carmen insulted her. Tyler hadn't mentioned anything when she had tutored him or when she was yelling at him. Hartley felt extra awful now.

"Yep. You're the reason she doesn't have a boyfriend or prom date anymore," Keisha told her with an enormous grin on her face.

"Why are you smiling? Carmen's determined to make my life miserable and all you can do is sit there and smile?" Hartley said irritably.

"Don't you see Hartley? He loves you, and now he's going to ask you to prom!" Keisha squealed.

"I don't think that's going to happen, Keisha. I said some things to Tyler that probably blew my chances of ever getting a date to the prom with him," Hartley admitted.

"I think you're wrong," Keisha sang out in a sing-song voice, still smiling.

"If I make it out of detention this afternoon it will be a miracle," Hartley sighed, wanting to change the subject.

"Do you want me to bust you out?" Keisha asked, barely containing her laughter.

"No, I think that might earn me another detention," Hartley said. The bell rang and they rose to go to class.

"I'll wait for you in the library, okay? You can tell me all about how traumatizing detention was." Keisha said as she and Hartley headed to their separate classes.

When her office aid hour finally came, Hartley got ready to pitch her prom idea to Principal Burns. He was getting ready to leave for lunch when Hartley knocked on his door.

"Hello, Hartley. What can I do for you?" Principal Burns asked.

"Well, sir, I had an idea about prom that I would like to discuss with you," Hartley said politely.

"Well let's hear it," Principal Burns said.

"I just think that it's so unfair that the elementary and middle school students are left out of prom," Hartley said.

"I don't think the high school prom is any place for small children," Principal Burns said.

"I agree. I think they should have their own prom. The middle school students could have it in the lunch room. The elementary kids could have theirs in the music room. Their parents could chaperone. We could sell tickets and triple the money we make on the high school prom," Hartley said.

"I don't know," Principal Burns said hesitantly.

"It would also boost Cainsville's economy. Think of the amount of dress, flower, and picture sales."

"It sounds like a good idea, but I'll have to talk it over with a few people," Principal Burns said. "What gave you the idea?"

"I just know how excited all the high school students get about prom. I just thought everyone should have that experience no matter what age they are," Hartley said smiling as sincerely as she could manage.

"You're a very thoughtful young lady, Hartley. I wish all the students were as considerate as you," Principal Burns said.

"Thank you, sir," Hartley said as she left the office. She crossed her fingers and hoped the idea worked.

Hartley did some paperwork during her office hour as she anticipated detention. She had no idea what went on in such places. Finally, the time came for her to make her way there. The room was filled with the miscreants of Cainsville High.

Hartley took the last available desk, located on the front row, next to a sophomore boy dressed completely in black. He was one of the two gothic kids that attended Cainsville High. He was wearing a dog collar with spikes, and Hartley thought she heard him growling. Hartley definitely felt out of place.

The teacher in charge, Coach Miles, was absentmindedly reading a newspaper. Kids were talking, throwing spit balls, and doing who knows what on the back row. Hartley tried to take out her Biology book to do some studying, but didn't think she would be able to accomplish that.

At that moment, Mr. Pooler walked by the classroom door. He was carrying what looked like a small fish tank. He passed the door way, but slowly backed up when he recognized Hartley in the sea of troublemakers. Hartley mouthed the words, "Help me" to him. Mr. Pooler then stepped into the classroom and cleared his throat.

Coach Miles didn't bother looking up. Then Mr. Pooler asked, "Coach Miles, do you mind if I borrow a student to help me with a science experiment?"

"Do whatever you want," said Coach Miles, still not bothering to look up from his paper.

"Hartley, come with me," Mr. Pooler said. Hartley grabbed her stuff and left the room as fast as she could. No one even noticed her leaving.

In the hallway, Hartley let out a sigh of relief. "Thanks, Mr. Pooler. I'm not sure I would have lasted an hour in there."

"You're welcome, Hartley. You can help me look for Arlene, the class tarantula. One of the freshmen let her escape, and I don't know where she is," Mr. Pooler said, which explained the tank he was carrying around.

"Sure," Hartley would happily look for a giant spider instead of sitting in detention.

"So, why were you in detention?" asked Mr. Pooler nonchalantly, but Hartley could tell he really wanted to know how she got there.

"Inappropriate word problem about a fellow student in math class," Hartley quoted the detention slip which she had to get signed by a parent or guardian.

"Ah," Mr. Pooler said. "Would this fellow student happen to be Carmen?"

"Yes," Hartley admitted as they continued to walk up and down the halls searching for the tarantula. "How did you guess?"

"I overheard Mr. Mercer talking about it in the teacher's lounge. He thought it was quite hilarious," Mr. Pooler told her.

"I'm glad he enjoyed it," Hartley said sarcastically.

"What happened, Hartley? You don't usually stoop to Carmen's level," Mr. Pooler asked her.

"I just lost it. I was so tired of her endless torture every day. I just wanted to show her what it felt like for once," Hartley confessed.

"You're a better person than she is, so don't let her bring you down," Mr. Pooler said reassuringly.

"Can we maybe change the subject, please? I really don't want to talk about Carmen anymore," Hartley asked.

"Sure. How's the scholarship application coming along?" Mr. Pooler asked.

Hartley hadn't given it much thought. She had filled out the information but was having trouble with the essay part of the application.

"Good. I'm just having a little trouble with the essay," Hartley said.

"What's the trouble? You're usually great at essays," Mr. Pooler asked.

"Well the topic is 'Why do you want to be a meteorologist?' I don't really want to be a meteorologist, and I'm only filling it out as backup plan. I can't exactly write that down, so I'm just stuck," Hartley admitted.

"Hartley, I want to tell you a story. When I was in high school, I knew a girl just like you. She was extremely smart, the smartest girl in the whole school. She wanted to go to college and become a lawyer. That's all she ever talked about becoming. She wanted to go to a fancy Ivy League school on the east coast. She had her entire future planned out." Mr. Pooler paused while Hartley wondered where the story was going but didn't interrupt.

"During our junior year of high school, there was a tornado. It was terrible, and it destroyed her family farm. Her family had to use all the money they had saved for her to go to college to rebuild the farm. Most people would have given up on the idea of going to college, but not her. She applied for every scholarship she could. She worked three jobs during her senior year and saved every penny she earned," Mr. Pooler paused.

"Did she make it to college?" Hartley asked interested in how the story ended.

"Yes, only not an Ivy League school. She went to a more affordable state college," Mr. Pooler said.

"Did she become a lawyer?" Hartley asked.

"No," Mr. Pooler said.

"No?" Hartley asked confused.

"No. She became a meteorologist," Mr. Pooler said.

"What?" Hartley asked curiously.

"You see, when that tornado hit and destroyed her home, it inspired her. She was angry at first. Angry that one tornado could cause so much

114

damage. Then she became curious. How did it do that? Why wasn't there any warning system? What could she do to put a stop to it?" Mr. Pooler told her. "She went on to become one of the leading meteorologists in the field. She helped design one of the early tornado warning systems."

"That's a great story, Mr. Pooler. Who was she?" Hartley asked.

"My wife," Mr. Pooler smiled as he said.

"What?" Hartley asked. She had known Mrs. Pooler before she passed away a few years ago from cancer but had no idea that she had lived such an interesting life.

"Helen went to the same college I did. We were friends in high school but didn't start dating until we were in college. She inspired me to be a science major, you know," Mr. Pooler admitted sheepishly.

"I had no idea Mrs. Pooler was a meteorologist," Hartley said.

"She used to chase tornadoes. I would chase with her during the summers when I wasn't teaching," Mr. Pooler said. "She kept chasing after she retired. She finally quit when she got sick."

They walked in silence for a moments remembering Mrs. Pooler. Then Hartley decided to ask the question she had been thinking. "Mr. Pooler, what exactly does this story have to do with me?"

"I know you have a plan for your future, Hartley, but sometimes life doesn't follow the plans we make," Mr. Pooler told her. "You have a very bright future ahead of you. I know you will do great things." Hartley felt a pang of emotion. Sometimes she felt like she was all alone, yet here was Mr. Pooler telling her that he believed in her. He continued, "Life is full of surprises. You never know what's going to happen next. Try not to make so many plans."

At that moment, Hartley saw Arlene, the tarantula, crawling off the locker and onto Mr. Pooler's shoulder. She pointed it out to Mr. Pooler, who quickly returned Arlene to her tank.

As they went their separate ways, Hartley called back to Mr. Pooler. "Mr. Pooler?" He turned around. "Thank you."

"For what?" Mr. Pooler asked.

"Always believing in me," Hartley simply said.

He smiled at her and said, "Anytime, Hartley, anytime," and walked away.

Chapter 10

Hartley found Keisha in the library and they made their way to Hartley's house. Hartley recounted the gruesome details of the few minutes she spent in detention and how Mr. Pooler rescued her.

"Could you keep the detention thing quiet for now? I'm not sure how my aunt and uncle are going to react," Hartley asked Keisha, knowing what a blabbermouth she was.

"Sure, Hartley, whatever you say," Keisha said rolling her eyes. Not a good sign, Hartley thought, knowing she would let it slip sooner or later.

As they walked up the front steps, they heard loud music blaring from the inside.

"What is that?" Keisha asked Hartley. Hartley just groaned and opened the door.

She found her aunt and uncle dancing around the kitchen. The old radio they kept in the kitchen to listen to farm reports was blasting out music from the oldies channel.

"What are you doing?" Hartley had to yell to be heard.

"Having a dance party! Come join us," Aunt Laura yelled back.

She wasn't sure what kind of dancing they were doing. Uncle Wyatt looked like he was having a seizure, and Aunt Laura looked like she was doing a combination of disco and hula dancing. Hartley sighed. All she had asked was for her aunt and uncle to act normal, and this is what she got. Keisha had already joined in the dancing. The only one not dancing was Hartley.

"Come on, Hartley!" They all shouted.

Hartley was about to refuse, but Keisha pulled her in. They danced around the kitchen for three more songs until they were all too tired to continue.

"So what do you think girls? Want us to chaperone your prom?" Uncle Wyatt asked.

"Yes!" Keisha said laughing.

"What about you, Hartley? You wouldn't be embarrassed of us, would you?" Uncle Wyatt asked.

"Go ahead. I'm not going," Hartley said.

"You have to. Prom is so much fun!" Aunt Laura said as she took a casserole out of the oven.

"I'm not going alone," Hartley said.

"You won't be alone, Hartley. You know Tyler's going to ask you because he dumped Carmen," Keisha blabbed.

"Oh, Hartley, you two will be so cute together, especially since you've had a crush on him for so many years," Aunt Laura gushed.

"We are not going together. No more prom talk!" Hartley snapped. Her lack of sleep was catching up to her.

They had all sat down at the table to eat. Hartley was glaring at all of them, daring them to say another word. Her aunt and uncle understood the look. After saying grace, their conversation changed direction.

"So girls, how was school today?" Aunt Laura asked thinking that would be a safe topic.

After Aunt Laura asked, Keisha burst into laughter. Uncle Wyatt and Aunt Laura looked confused. Hartley decided she better tell them about her detention.

"Well, I got detention today," Hartley confessed.

"What?" Aunt Laura asked, looking shocked and delighted. "Oh, thank God! We thought you'd never do anything bad! You are a normal girl!"

Uncle Wyatt didn't say a word. Instead, he got up from the table and looked out the window, which prompted Hartley to ask, "Uncle Wyatt, what are you doing?"

"Looking for the flying pigs," Uncle Wyatt replied. This was too much for Keisha to handle, and she almost chocked from laughing so hard.

Once Uncle Wyatt returned to the table, Hartley took her detention slip out of her pocket to show them.

"An inappropriate word problem about a fellow student?" They read it aloud and then broke into laughter.

"Hartley, I thought we raised you better," Uncle Wyatt choked out between fits of laughter.

"Yes, Hartley, I never thought you would do something as horrible as…what was it? Telling an inappropriate word problem? I am ashamed." Aunt Laura pretended to scold. Keisha had actually fallen out of her chair from laughing so hard.

"I'm glad you all think it's funny, because I don't," Hartley told them sternly.

"We're just joking, Hartley, tell us what really happened," Aunt Laura said.

After Hartley told them the whole story, they only laughed harder. They signed her detention slip and started sharing stories about all the things they received detention for in high school. They even shared a story about Hartley's dad getting detention on his first day of school. Hartley realized her one detention was nothing compared to her aunt and uncle's detentions or even her dad's.

After washing the dishes, Keisha and Hartley went upstairs to Hartley's room to work on their homework. Hartley spotted the notebook full of her prom plans and quickly stuffed it into her book bag. She didn't want Keisha to find it and start asking questions. Thankfully Keisha didn't notice, so Hartley didn't have to explain.

"Hey, can I look at your Spanish homework? I think I might have accidently mistranslated 'grandma' as 'meatball,'" Keisha asked.

"Sure," Hartley said, handing Keisha her Spanish homework.

Hartley crashed on her bed and was soon joined by Bob Dylan, while Keisha sat at her desk and worked on her Spanish homework. Hartley was exhausted from the early start and the tiring day she had. She had just closed her eyes when she heard Keisha say, "Hartley?"

"Hmm?" Hartley mumbled, not wanting to get up.

"I think someone is trying to get your attention," Keisha said.

"What are you talking about?" Hartley asked when she heard a tiny clinking sound coming from her window. A few seconds later, she heard it again. She walked over to her window and opened it. It was too dark to tell who was down there. A few seconds later a pebble came flying through the window and hit her in the head.

"Ow!" Hartley said.

"Hartley?" a confused voice asked from below.

"Tyler? What are you doing?" Hartley yelled out her window, instantly recognizing the voice.

121

"I need to talk to you," Tyler asked.

"Now?" Hartley asked.

"Yes. Please, it will only take a second," Tyler begged.

"Fine. I'll be down there in a minute," Hartley said as she closed her window. Her head was hurting from where she got hit. Keisha was just sitting there like she was watching the most romantic movie of her life.

"What?" Hartley asked.

"He's going to ask you to prom. Your dreams are finally coming true," Keisha said in that same sing-song voice from lunch.

"Would you shut up!" Hartley grimaced as she walked out the door and went downstairs.

Aunt Laura and Uncle Wyatt were in the kitchen as she headed for the front door.

"Where are you going?" Aunt Laura asked. They were curious; Hartley hardly ever left the house at night because she believed that time should be spent studying.

"I have to go talk to Tyler. I'll be back soon," Hartley said.

"Why are you holding your head like that?" Uncle Wyatt asked curiously.

"He was throwing rocks at my window and hit me in the head with one," Hartley explained.

"Isn't that the sweetest thing you've ever heard, Wyatt?" Aunt Laura gushed, sounding an awful lot like Keisha.

"I'll be back soon." Hartley rolled her eyes as she walked out the door. Maybe their house had a gas leak.

The sky was dark, but the stars were shining brightly. Hartley found Tyler waiting for her under her window. Hartley noticed he was holding flowers.

"I'm sorry. I didn't mean to hit you in the head. I just wanted to talk to you," Tyler apologized, handing Hartley the flowers. It was a bouquet of sunflowers, her favorite.

"Thanks," Hartley said taking the flowers. "Next time you need to talk - just call."

They stood there in silence for a moment when they both said at the same time, "I'm sorry."

Hartley started to speak but Tyler spoke first. "I'm sorry for what I said, Hartley."

"No, you were right. I have no business giving advice on relationships," Hartley replied.

"Still, I shouldn't have said anything. I was angry, and I said things I didn't mean," Tyler said.

"I'm sorry. I wasn't really mad at you. I was just taking my anger out on you," Hartley said.

Tyler was about to speak again when they heard a voice from above shout, "Stop apologizing, and get to the good stuff!"

"What the…?" Tyler said. Hartley rolled her eyes and yelled, "Keisha, a little privacy please!"

"I'm not the idiots talking under an open window!" Keisha yelled back.

"Do you have another rock?" Hartley asked Tyler. Tyler motioned for Hartley to follow him. They walked away from the house out of sight and hopefully out of earshot.

"Sorry about her. She's too nosey for her own good," Hartley said.

"What was the part about getting to the good stuff?" Tyler asked.

"Keisha has this crazy idea that since you broke up with Carmen, you're going to ask me to prom," Hartley's face blushed as she said it.

"It doesn't sound that crazy," Tyler said.

Hartley looked down at the flowers in her hand and remembered what Tyler had said. "Oh. No," Hartley said shaking her head.

"No?" Tyler asked, looking confused and hurt.

"No. I mean, yes, I would love to go with you, but no it's a horrible idea," Hartley explained.

"Why is it a horrible idea?"

"Because you just broke up with Carmen, and you're upset. You're not thinking clearly," Hartley insisted.

"I'm not that upset. Breaking up with Carmen is the smartest thing I've done in a long time. I'm finally seeing clearly," Tyler said.

Hartley had waited for this moment for a long time but wasn't sure she was ready to handle it. She wanted to believe what Tyler was saying was true, but didn't know if she could. "Everyone will think I'm just your second choice and that you had to settle for me," Hartley argued.

"No one could possibly think that about you. I don't just want to go to prom with you. I want to be your boyfriend. I've wanted that for a long time, but I wasn't sure if you felt the same way. I was afraid of change, but you made me realize that change is okay," Tyler said.

"Really?" Hartley squeaked.

"Yes, really," Tyler said smiling at her.

That was all Hartley needed to hear. She ran and threw her arms around Tyler and kissed him. Tyler picked her up off the ground and twirled her around. Hartley felt like she was going to explode with happiness. It was her first real kiss and could not have been more perfect.

"I take that as a yes," Tyler said still hugging her.

"Yes, that's a yes," Hartley said smiling. As she leaned in to kiss him again, Hartley heard a familiar barking coming from behind. She turned around to see Bob Dylan watching the couple suspiciously.

"We're never going to be alone are we?" Tyler asked. Hartley laughed and shook her head. Tyler held her hand as he walked her home. Bob Dylan walked in front of them and stopped every so often to make sure they were following him.

When they got to the house, they said goodnight. Hartley didn't dare kiss Tyler goodnight because she knew there was a house full of people and an overprotective golden retriever watching. Surprisingly everyone had gone to bed by the time she got inside. Hartley was so tired from her exciting day that she fell asleep immediately.

Hartley was the last one up the next morning. Aunt Laura was already serving bacon and eggs by the time Hartley made it to the table.

As Hartley sat down, Uncle Wyatt was the first one to speak. "So, Hartley, did you have fun kissing the neighbor boy last night?" Aunt Laura and Keisha burst out in laughter as Hartley groaned.

"You were watching me? Has anyone in this house heard of privacy?" Hartley asked mortified.

"If you want privacy, you'll have to go to the cornfield like your Aunt Laura and I do," Uncle Wyatt said.

"Eww," Hartley said as Keisha continued laughing.

"Well, I think it's sweet. I always thought you and Tyler would make an adorable couple," Aunt Laura gushed.

"I knew it. I told you, Hartley," Keisha gloated.

Hartley grinned and sheepishly announced, "Well, in case you didn't overhear last night, Tyler is now my boyfriend," although everyone at the table already seemed to know. "And we are going to the prom together."

"I knew it!" Keisha exclaimed.

"That's nice," Uncle Wyatt said.

"Really?" Aunt Laura said, looking positively ecstatic.

"Yes," Hartley said suspiciously.

"Wait here. I have a surprise," Aunt Laura said as she ran upstairs. A few moments later she returned carrying a garment bag.

"I wasn't sure you were going to go, but I made it just in case," Aunt Laura said as she unzipped the bag.

Inside was a beautiful prom dress. The dress was short and made of bright blue gingham material. It had a sweetheart neckline outlined in red sequins. There were sequins around the waist and hem. Underneath the skirt, Aunt Laura had added matching blue tulle to make the dress poof out. It was beyond perfect. Hartley couldn't imagine a better dress. She was speechless.

"I know it's not from a store, but I thought you would like it. I was inspired by *The Wizard of Oz*. I know it's your favorite book and movie," Aunt Laura looked worried that Hartley didn't like the dress.

Hartley got up from the table and hugged her aunt. "It's the most beautiful dress ever. Thank you," Hartley was touched that her aunt would go to so much trouble to make her dress.

Aunt Laura breathed a sigh of relief. "I've been working on it for weeks."

"Is that why you were acting so strange the other day?" Hartley asked.

"Yes. I wanted it to be a surprise," Aunt Laura confessed.

"It's the best surprise anyone could get," Hartley said.

"I'll hang it in your closet. You can try it on this afternoon when you get home," Aunt Laura said. Hartley thought she saw tears in her aunt's eyes.

Hartley and Keisha finished breakfast and got ready for school. As they walked out the door Uncle Wyatt said, "You girls have a good day at school. Hartley, try to stay out of detention, and no more kissing your boyfriend in public."

Hartley rolled her eyes and left for school. On the way, she discussed prom plans with Keisha. For the first time, Hartley felt excited about the prom, instead of the constant ominous feeling in the pit of her stomach. *"Everything is going to be okay,"* Hartley allowed herself think, if only for a little while.

Hartley said goodbye to Keisha as she went to Calculus. She found Tyler sitting in the back next to her desk. She tried to ignore the stares they were getting from their fellow classmates, especially the evil looks Carmen was shooting their way.

The morning announcements came on the television in the room. Principal Burns went through the usual mundane messages. Finally he said, "In addition to the high school prom, the elementary and middle schools will also be having their own proms Saturday night. This is a new idea we are trying out and hope to make it a new tradition."

Hartley couldn't believe her idea worked. She didn't realize she was smiling until Tyler whispered, "Why are you smiling?"

"I was just thinking how cute the little kids will look in their prom outfits," Hartley said lamely. She had no idea what Tyler would think if he only knew the truth.

"Okay," Tyler said suspiciously. Thankfully, Mr. Mercer started grilling them with questions. At the end of class he announced he was giving a test Monday morning. The class grumbled in unison. No one was ready for the test.

"Hartley?" Tyler asked as they walked to their next class.

"Yes, I'll help you study," Hartley answered reading his mind.

Tyler smiled. He loved how she knew what he was going to ask without having to actually ask. "How about today in the library before my game?"

"Sure," Hartley said.

The day passed smoothly for Hartley. She was sad to leave Tyler as he went to history class and she went to the office. She was looking forward to studying with him in the library after school. Her office hour passed slowly, as she organized the filing cabinet. She was relieved to hear the bell ring.

She quickly made her way to the library where she found Tyler already waiting for her. They were the only people in the library besides the old librarian. Most students didn't spend Friday afternoon in the library, but both Hartley and Tyler knew they had to study if they wanted to pass Calculus.

As she sat down at the secluded table in the back of the library, her book bag fell open dumping the entire contents onto the floor. She had been meaning to clean it out, but always forgot. Tyler helped her pick up the discarded books and notebooks. Hartley was too busy to notice that the notebook that held the names of everyone in

Cainsville and her ideas to get them out of town had fallen open, and Tyler had picked it up.

"Hartley?" Tyler asked.

"Yeah?" Hartley asked, stuffing one of her many books back into the bag.

"Why do you have everyone's name written in a notebook?" Tyler asked curiously.

"Um…" Hartley stammered. She searched her mind for reasonable explanation, but her mind was blank.

"History project?" Hartley blurted out.

"You don't take history," Tyler said shaking his head.

Hartley took a deep breath and decided for the first time in her life to share her secret. She was tired of hiding who she really was. If she couldn't trust Tyler, her boyfriend, one of her oldest friends, who could she trust? She looked around to make sure they were alone. She sat down and motioned for Tyler to do the same.

"I know what I'm about to tell you is going to sound really strange, but promise me you won't freak out," Hartley told Tyler calmly.

Tyler looked worried. "What is it Hartley? Are you a serial killer? Is this a list of who you're going to kill?"

"No, I'm not a serial killer," Hartley said as Tyler let out a sigh of relief.

Hartley continued, "You know how my parents died, right?" Tyler nodded his head. "Well, ever since I survived the tornado that killed my parents, I've had these, um, visions of when tornadoes are going to hit."

"Visions?" Tyler asked curiously.

"Yes, visions; only of tornadoes, though. They're like warnings. I see a specific person getting hurt or dying in a tornado, and then I figure out how to save them," Hartley explained.

"So, you have a vision of a person dying in a tornado then you save them and change the future?" Tyler asked, slowly comprehending.

"Yes," Hartley said.

"What are your visions like?" Tyler asked.

"Remember the other night when we were arguing and I passed out?" Hartley asked him.

He nodded. "You don't have low blood sugar?"

"No," Hartley said.

"Who did you see in your vision?" Tyler asked.

"Everyone at prom, then the entire town," Hartley said.

"A tornado is going to hit during prom?" Tyler asked.

"Yes," Hartley said. "And that's my list of people I need to get out of town."

132

"Well, we should warn everybody, make sure they get somewhere safe," Tyler said standing up.

"No, Tyler, sit down," Hartley said, grabbing his arm and forcing him to sit down.

"But we have to help, Hartley," Tyler said.

"I know, I'm going to, Tyler," Hartley said. "But, I can't go running around town telling people I have psychic visions of tornadoes. No one will believe me."

"I believe you," Tyler said.

"I know, but you're special. Not everyone is like you. They'll want to know how I know a tornado is going to hit when the forecast hasn't even predicted bad weather for that day. They'll say I'm crazy and send me to a mental institution," Hartley said.

"I guess you're right," Tyler said. "So, how can I help get…"he said looking at the list of people, "pretty much everyone out of town next Saturday without them knowing what we're doing?"

Hartley leaned over and kissed Tyler on the cheek.

"What was that for?" Tyler asked.

"For being you," Hartley said.

Hartley and Tyler continued talking and finally studying. They never noticed that someone was standing behind the bookshelf listening to their entire conversation. Carmen couldn't believe what

she was hearing. She also couldn't wait to tell the
entire school what she had heard.

Chapter 11

When Hartley got home, Aunt Laura was waiting for her with the mail. Hartley saw several letters from different colleges, but not one from Stanford. Aunt Laura helped her open them. Hartley was pleased to see that she had been accepted to all of them, including the University of Oklahoma, but was still worried that her Stanford letter had not arrived.

"Congratulations, sweetheart, I'm so proud of you. Look at all these schools you got into," Aunt Laura said.

"Thanks," Hartley said, frowning.

"What's wrong?" Aunt Laura said.

"I didn't get a letter from Stanford, and if I do get one, I think it might be a rejection," Hartley confessed.

"Hartley, you're going to get in. Don't worry about it. Even if you don't get in, not that you won't, you have all these great options," Aunt Laura said. "I mean look at this one," she said as she pushed the acceptance letter from OU forward. "It's close to home. You could come home and visit on the weekends."

Hartley smiled. "I will miss you, wherever I go, you know that, right?"

Aunt Laura smiled at her. "Yes, and I'll miss you too. I worry about you going all the way to California to college."

"You know why I want to go there don't you?" Hartley asked her aunt.

"I know, and I don't blame you, Hartley," Aunt Laura said. "I would want to leave Kansas as fast as possible if I saw all the things you do. But California is so far away."

"Is it strange that I want to go there because my mom and dad went there, too?" Hartley asked.

"That's perfectly understandable. But your parents would be proud of you no matter where you go to college," Aunt Laura said.

"If I do get into Stanford, I'll come home for holidays and summers," Hartley said reassuringly.

"I know you will, but I'll still miss you. I'm used to seeing you every day, not a couple of weeks out of the a year," Aunt Laura said.

Hartley suddenly realized how much she was going to miss her life in Kansas. She loved her aunt and uncle and had never really spent much time away from home. She was definitely going to miss Bob Dylan. What about Keisha and Tyler? Was she really ready to say goodbye to them? Stanford was her dream college and California was ideal for weather, but what about everything she would be leaving behind?

At dinner that night, Hartley told her aunt and uncle that Tyler knew about her visions. They were surprised and concerned, but Hartley explained the situation. She knew she could trust Tyler. They eventually agreed, and then they all turned their attention to the upcoming tornado.

They needed a game plan to get everyone somewhere safe. Their main problem was getting the people who didn't have a reason for being at school on prom night out of town. Prom was a big deal in Cainsville and usually the entire family came to watch the students make a grand entrance. The people Hartley was most concerned about getting out of town were older and had no school-age children. Brainstorming ways to get them out was not an easy process.

"Any ideas?" Hartley asked hopefully.

"No," Aunt Laura sighed.

"Nope," Uncle Wyatt said.

"Let's go over the current plan. All elementary, middle, and high school students will be at school. The elementary kids will be having their prom in the music room which is made of solid concrete blocks and should be safe. The middle school students will be having their prom in the lunch room, also made out of concrete. The high school prom will be in the gym which is not safe. During prom, I'm going to sneak into the office and pull the tornado alarm. That will give the high

137

school a chance to get to the locker room. I signed you two up as chaperones. You can help get the people to safety. Got it?" Hartley asked.

Her aunt and uncle nodded. Hartley stared at her handwritten list. She realized it would be easier to divide the women and men into two groups and think of ways to get them out of town. Finally an idea came to her.

"Fishing," Hartley blurted out.

"What?" Aunt Laura and Uncle Wyatt said simultaneously.

"Uncle Wyatt, can you convince all the men on this list to go on a fishing trip next Saturday?" Hartley asked.

"I guess so. It shouldn't be that difficult," Uncle Wyatt said looking over the list.

"Now all we need is an idea for the women," Hartley said.

"What about this, Hartley?" Aunt Laura asked holding up a newspaper.

There was an ad for a women's conference in Topeka for the following Saturday.

"That's perfect!" Hartley said. "Now we just have to convince everyone to go."

"I'll show this to Bertha Jones at church Sunday. She'll have all the women in town going." Aunt Laura said. Bertha Jones was the town's busybody and took pride in organizing events and forcing people into group activities.

"Good idea. Tell her that the women need something to do because all the men are going fishing," Hartley said. She felt like everything might actually work out.

"What about the Richards? You know that they never leave town," Uncle Wyatt pointed out.

"That is a problem," Hartley said. Hartley thought how to get the Richards out of town. They were an elderly couple that rarely left their farm. Then Hartley had an idea.

"Emily," Hartley said.

"What about her?" Uncle Wyatt asked.

"The Richards would leave Cainsville to visit Emily," Hartley explained. Emily was the Richards' only granddaughter. They raised Emily after her mom abandoned her. Emily was only four years older than Hartley and one of the few people that was actually nice to Hartley. Mrs. Richards just told Hartley that Emily got a job in Seattle after graduating from college.

"I could call Emily and tell her that her grandparents seem lonely and need a vacation. Maybe suggest that she invite them to Seattle for the weekend," Hartley prompted.

"It could work," Uncle Wyatt said.

"How are you going to get everyone to prom on time?" Aunt Laura asked.

"I've taken care of that. I added this to the announcements for Monday morning," Hartley said, showing them a copy of the announcement sheet for Monday. The sheet stated that everyone should be at the gym by 6:30 for the grand entrance that would take place at 7:00 sharp. No one would be admitted after seven.

"Won't the office be locked? How are you going to get to the alarm?" Uncle Wyatt asked.

"I'll use my key. Mrs. Phillips gave it to me for being the office aide," Hartley said.

"What about everyone at the hospital, fire department, and police station?" Aunt Laura said.

"Everyone at the hospital should be fine. The state of Kansas has strict building codes for hospitals. The fire department has a storm shelter, so everyone on call will be safe. The jail cells in the police stations are made out of cement, so all the officers working Saturday night will be safe."

"What about the first vision you had? The one where you were driving," Aunt Laura asked.

"I guess that's what would have happened if I wasn't going to prom. But it should be fine now since I'm going," Hartley reasoned.

"Sounds like you have it all figured out," Uncle Wyatt said.

"I think so," Hartley said. "I guess we'll see next Saturday."

Over the weekend, the three with help from Tyler began working on their plan. Surprisingly, everything went according to plan. Uncle Wyatt was able to convince the men that Saturday would be the perfect day for fishing. Aunt Laura mentioned how interesting the women's conference sounded, and Bertha Jones took the bait. Hartley was ecstatic when Mrs. Richards told her at church that they had received an invitation to visit Emily the following weekend. All the plans they had made seemed to be falling into place.

Chapter 12

Monday morning arrived and found Hartley in a good mood. The cloud of doom that had been hanging over her head had disappeared. She felt certain that everything was working in her favor. She was ready to tackle her Calculus test and was sure that Tyler was ready for his Calculus test, too. She was confident that no one would be dying on prom night and had a strange feeling that her acceptance letter from Stanford was in the mail.

Hartley was late to school. She had made the mistake of trying to style her untamable hair and that had cost her some time. She noticed there were still people in the hallway, so she had time to make it to class. As she walked down the hallway, Hartley sensed that people were staring at her. She became paranoid that people were talking about her. She looked down at her outfit. She was wearing a dress and sweater, nothing unusual. She didn't have toilet paper stuck to her shoe. She tried to tell herself it was all in her imagination, but she couldn't shake it.

When she rounded the corner, Hartley found Carmen standing in front of her locker. When she saw Hartley, she smiled which was very strange behavior for Carmen.

"Hello, Hartley," Carmen said in her sickly sweet voice that was as fake as her nose.

"Hello," Hartley said as she got her books out of her locker.

"Did you have a nice weekend?" Carmen asked nicely.

"Yes?" Harley answered. She wasn't sure what Carmen was up to and it made her very nervous.

"Really? Are you sure you didn't have any visions of tornadoes?" Carmen asked in her sweet voice.

"What did you say?" Hartley stammered horrified.

"You heard me. I know all about your 'visions'," Carmen said using air quotes.

"No," Hartley said shaking her head in denial. "No, you can't."

"But I do. You know who told me?" Carmen asked.

Hartley just stood there still shaking her head.

"Tyler. He thought it was really funny. He came over this weekend, and we had a nice laugh about it," Carmen said cruelly.

"You're lying," Hartley squeaked.

"No, I'm not," Carmen said. "And Tyler thought it was hilarious when I told the entire school about your delusional little visions. They thought it was hysterical. I always knew you were weird, Hartley, but I had no idea what a complete freak you are."

Carmen walked away, leaving Hartley frozen in place. She wasn't being paranoid. Everyone was talking about her. She couldn't believe this was actually happening. She felt sick. Hartley heard the bell ring and slowly began walking to class. She knew she should turn around and run home, but she had a test to take. Mr. Mercer wouldn't care if her life was ending. He would probably give her detention if she was late for class.

During class, Hartley could tell that Tyler was trying to get her attention, but she stayed focused on her test. She was devastated. She had made a huge mistake in trusting him. Hartley never would have thought Tyler was capable of betraying her like that, but she wasn't sure what to think anymore.

Hartley rushed out of math class after the test was over. Unfortunately for her, Tyler followed.

"Wait, Hartley, wait!" Tyler yelled after her, as she continued to walk to her next class. Finally she stopped at her locker and allowed him to speak.

"You have to believe me, I didn't tell anyone. I don't know how everyone found out, but I didn't do it," Tyler told her.

"You told Carmen and she told the entire school. That's how everyone knows. I can't believe you would do that. I trusted you," Hartley said angrily.

"I would never tell her. I swear. You have to believe me. What can I do to prove it to you?" Tyler begged.

"You can stay away from me. I never want to talk to you ever again. Got it?" Hartley said.

"But…" Tyler began to say, but Hartley walked away.

The bell rang, but Hartley wasn't concerned with being late to class. At the end of the hall she saw Keisha and felt a wave of relief. If there was one person who would understand, it would be her best friend. She would help Hartley through all of this.

"I'm so glad to see you," Hartley said. Keisha, however, did not look happy to see Hartley. In fact, she looked quite the opposite.

"Is it true?" Keisha asked Hartley.

"Is what true?" Hartley asked.

"You know what? Everyone's talking about the visions you think you have," Keisha said.

"Yes," Hartley said reluctantly.

"Why didn't you tell me? I thought I was your best friend. Is that why you act so strange all the time?" Keisha shouted at Hartley.

"You don't understand, I wanted to tell you, but I couldn't," Hartley tried to explain, but Keisha wasn't listening.

"Why couldn't you tell me? You don't trust me, is that it?" Keisha asked defensively.

"No, of course, I trust you, I just…" Hartley was lost for words.

"That's what I thought," Keisha said as she walked away.

"I didn't tell you because I was afraid this would happen," Hartley whispered to herself.

The next three classes were terrible for Hartley. Instead of the whispers and pointing, her classmates had taken to laughing loudly or shouting rude remarks at her. Hartley wondered if she could try and convince them Carmen was lying, but she figured it was pointless. No one would take her word over Carmen's. Hartley endured their ridiculing in silence. She ate lunch alone in the bathroom. She was counting down the minutes until school was over and she could leave.

As she made her way to Advanced Biology, Hartley took a deep breath. This was her last class with other students; if she made it through the class, she should be okay. However, as soon as she walked in the door, she knew it was not going to be okay. Everyone seemed to have something to say to her.

"Hey, Hartley, how's the weather looking?"

"See any tornadoes lately?"

Hartley sat down and tried to ignore them. She glanced over and saw Carmen smiling and Tyler avoiding eye contact with her.

At that point, Mr. Pooler entered the room. "That's quite enough; I want everyone to be quiet. If I hear another comment, it'll be detention."

Mr. Pooler handed out a pop quiz over the weather topics they had been studying. It was too much for the class to handle and Hartley heard someone from the back of the class shout, "Hartley, I bet you didn't see that coming!"

Before Mr. Pooler could speak, Hartley had stood up. She was done with their comments and laughing.

"It's true, all of it. I have premonitions of people dying in tornadoes, and I save them. It started after my parents died and I survived. I know most of you think I'm a freak and I'm making it all up, but I can prove it."

Hartley continued. "Chesney, remember when you got locked in the bathroom and you're parents had to come looking for you? Amazing, wasn't it, how your house was leveled by a tornado and your family wasn't hurt? I was the one who locked you in the bathroom." Chesney looked shocked.

"Ashley, isn't it too much of a coincidence how your grandparents weren't home when that tornado wiped out their farm? Isn't it interesting how they mysteriously "won" that vacation? I made that happen."

Hartley continued going around the room and listing examples. She had helped almost every single student or a family member in some way. Finally, Hartley turned around to face Mr. Pooler. "Remember a few weeks ago, when your car wouldn't start? I did that, too. I saw you driving off a bridge trying to outrun a tornado. You got trapped in your car and drowned."

Mr. Pooler looked astonished and the class was speechless. Hartley didn't bother waiting for anyone to regain their speech. She grabbed her book bag and ran out of the room. She was tired and was going home. She didn't care if she didn't have permission or if she got detention. She didn't really care about anything anymore.

She was halfway down the hall when she heard someone calling her name. She turned around to see Mr. Pooler following her.

"I'm sorry Mr. Pooler, but I can't take it anymore. Please don't make me go back in there," Hartley pleaded, on the verge of tears.

"No, Hartley, I won't make you go back. I just wanted to make sure you were okay," Mr. Pooler said kindly.

"Well, I've had better days," Hartley said.

"Is all that stuff you said in class true?" Mr. Pooler asked.

Hartley didn't say a word. Instead, she reached into her book bag and pulled out the proof she knew Mr. Pooler needed to believe her story. She handed him the spark plugs she stole from his car.

Mr. Pooler started laughing. "I guess I owe you a big thank you."

"You don't have to thank me. It's just part of my job," Hartley explained.

"It can't be easy for you. What can I do to help?" Mr. Pooler asked.

"A tornado is going to hit Saturday during prom," Hartley said. "I don't know exactly what Carmen told everyone, but I'll need help getting everyone out of the gym and into the locker rooms when it hits."

"I'm chaperoning. I can help you do that," Mr. Pooler said.

"Thanks, Mr. Pooler. Can I go home now?" Hartley asked.

"Yes, take this," Mr. Pooler said, scribbling onto a piece of paper and handing Hartley an excuse so she could leave early.

"Thanks," Hartley said and left school as fast as she could.

Chapter 13

Hartley didn't go home. She didn't feel like explaining everything to her aunt and uncle just yet. Instead she opted to drive aimlessly around town. Hartley wasn't paying much attention to where she was going and found herself driving a lone stretch of highway, miles outside of Cainsville.

Hartley stopped when she reached Harper's field, the place where her parents had died. She didn't know what she was doing there, but it felt like the right place to be. She got out of the truck and began walking through the green grass that covered the field. The sky was filled with fluffy clouds with the sun hiding behind them. There was a gentle breeze blowing. Hartley lay down on the grass and looked up at the sky. She suddenly had the urge to talk to her parents. She looked around sheepishly, but she knew she was completely alone. Not a single car had passed since she had been there.

She took a deep breath and started talking. "I never got a chance to know you, but I really wish you were here right now. My life isn't going so well, and I don't know what to do. Don't get me wrong, Aunt Laura and Uncle Wyatt are doing a great job, but I can't help but wish you were here with me or wish that I was up there with you." At that moment the sun burst through a cloud and a ray of sunlight hit Hartley directly in the face. She knew it was a message from her parents. It made her feel a little better, and she decided to head home.

When she got home, she found Uncle Wyatt and Aunt Laura waiting for her. She figured someone from the school had called them. Then Hartley noticed they were smiling.

"What's going on?" Hartley asked.

"Your Stanford letter came," Aunt Laura said, handing Hartley an envelope.

"Really? That's the best news I've had all day. You wouldn't believe the day I had. I really need something good to happen," Hartley said as she ripped the envelope open and unfolded the letter. She looked at the first sentence, which read, "We regret to inform you.."

She didn't bother reading the rest. Her dream college didn't want her. Uncle Wyatt and Aunt Laura must have noticed the disappointment in her face, because Aunt Laura said, "Hartley, I'm so sorry." But Hartley wasn't listening. She threw the letter on the floor and ran outside.

Laura and Wyatt stood there. Wyatt picked the letter off the floor. "I can't believe she didn't get in. There must be some mistake."

"What are we going to do? She's devastated," Laura asked her husband.

"I'll go talk to her," Wyatt said. Laura nodded in response and said, "I'll make her something special to eat. Maybe that will cheer her up."

Wyatt went outside to look for Hartley. He searched everywhere, and was about to give up when he noticed Bob Dylan sitting at the base of the windmill looking up. Hartley was sitting on top of the old windmill that sat in the middle of their field.

"Hartley! Don't jump. Come down from there. Everything's going to be okay!" Wyatt shouted. He knew Hartley was upset, but he didn't really think she was so upset that she was going to kill herself.

"I'm not going to jump! I'm just stuck," Hartley shouted back down at him.

"Why did you climb the windmill if you're afraid of heights?" Wyatt asked.

"I don't know! It seemed like a good place to think," Hartley shouted back down.

"I'm coming up there," Wyatt said.

When Wyatt climbed the top of the windmill, he found Hartley crying. He put his arm around her shoulder and asked her, "What's wrong?"

"Everything," Hartley said.

"Come on, it can't be that bad," Uncle Wyatt said.

"It is. Tyler told Carmen about my visions, and she told the whole school. I lost my only chance of having a boyfriend, and my best friend hates me. Everyone else thinks I'm a freak, and to top it all off, I just got rejected by the school of my dreams," Hartley said.

"That does sound pretty bad, but it's not the end of the world," Uncle Wyatt said. "You may not have been accepted by the school you wanted, but you got a whole pile of great schools that want you. You will have plenty of chances to have a boyfriend. If you couldn't trust the stupid neighbor boy, you're better off without him. Your best friend won't hate you forever. Everyone might think you're a freak, but who cares what everyone else thinks? You're a beautiful, smart, funny girl."

"But this wasn't how it was supposed to be. I had a plan," Hartley mumbled through the stream of tears.

"Funny how life never follows the plans we make for ourselves. When I moved to Cainsville to live with my grandparents, the only thing I planned on was getting out of here and never coming back. I was an angry kid. I was angry that my dad bailed on me and that my mom gave up and shipped me off to live with my grandparents."

"I used to be goofball. I used to pull pranks and get in trouble all the time. I figured if I made people laugh, they wouldn't see how hurt I was. It wasn't until I met your dad, that I straightened my life out. When I wasn't going to graduate, he helped me study. When I couldn't get into college, he told me to join the army. George was the first real friend I ever had."

"Really?" Hartley asked. She had never heard this story before.

"Really. He made me realize that Cainsville was my home and that people actually cared about me. That's why we came back here. That wasn't in my plan. Then your parents moved back, too, and they had you. We were all so happy."

"When your parents died, I was so angry. It wasn't in the plan. We were all supposed to grow older together. But when George and Sarah died, they gave me the greatest gift of my life. They gave me you. I never planned on raising you, but it's been the best surprise of my life."

Hartley was crying now for a different reason. She realized she loved her aunt and uncle like they were her actual parents.

"Don't try to plan your life, Hartley, because it's full of surprises," Uncle Wyatt said and Hartley nodded in agreement. He helped her climb down the windmill. Uncle Wyatt's words were sweet and sincere, but she still felt lost.

Over dinner, Hartley explained what happened during her day. Her aunt and uncle were very understanding. When Hartley begged them to let her stay home from school until the prom was over, they didn't have the heart to say no. Hartley had never missed school, so if she was begging to stay home, it was for a good reason. Compared to the amount of school her classmates missed, four days was nothing.

Her time at home didn't help Hartley feel better. She had fallen into a depression that she couldn't shake. Apparently, her aunt and uncle noticed because they began hiding all the sharp objects. Hartley tried to explain she wasn't suicidal, but couldn't successfully convince them.

To make matters worse, townspeople kept calling the house, telling Aunt Laura or Uncle Wyatt they should have Hartley committed. It happened again on Friday night while they were trying to eat dinner. Uncle Wyatt made the mistake of answering the phone. Hartley and Aunt Laura watched as he hung up, slamming the phone down in anger.

"Don't people in this town have anything better to do?" Uncle Wyatt asked furiously as he sat down.

"They're so hateful," Aunt Laura said.

"Maybe they're right. Maybe I should be in a mental institution," Hartley said darkly.

"No, Hartley, don't you dare think that. You are special. You use your gift to help people," Aunt Laura said.

"Are you telling me that you never once considered that maybe I would be better off in a place like that?" Hartley asked.

"No. You belong right here with us. Cainsville is your home as much as it is theirs," Uncle Wyatt said.

"Maybe I should stop helping people then," Hartley suggested bitterly.

"Okay," Uncle Wyatt said.

"What?" Aunt Laura asked.

"Stop helping people. Let them see what it's like without your help," Uncle Wyatt said.

"People would die. I can't do that," Hartley said.

"Wyatt, why would you say that?" Aunt Laura asked.

"To remind Hartley why she does it. To help people, even when it's hard, because it's the right thing to do."

"Doing the right thing isn't always easy," Hartley sighed.

"I guess you're not going to the prom tomorrow night are you?" Aunt Laura asked.

"No, but you two are. You'll take my key and get into the principal's office. Pull the alarm and make sure everyone's safe. Mr. Pooler will help you," Hartley said.

"What about you? Where will you be?" Aunt Laura asked.

"Safe in the storm cellar with Bob Dylan," Hartley responded, but she had something entirely different planned.

Chapter 14

Hartley lounged around the house Saturday. She knew that she should be getting ready for prom like the rest of her classmates. She knew she should be doing her hair and makeup and putting on her amazing dress. Instead she was sitting of the couch with Bob Dylan, rereading *The Wizard of Oz* for the hundredth time.

When Aunt Laura and Uncle Wyatt came downstairs, Hartley was stunned. She had never seen her aunt and uncle dressed up. Aunt Laura was wearing a short black dress and Uncle Wyatt was wearing a suit. They looked great.

"You look amazing," Hartley said.

"Are you sure you don't want to come with us, Hartley? I feel a little strange chaperoning a prom when my own kid isn't there," Uncle Wyatt asked.

"Sorry, I don't think I can," Hartley replied.

"I laid your dress on your bed in case you change your mind," Aunt Laura said.

"You should get going. You don't want to be late," Hartley said as she ushered them out the door.

"You're sure you'll be safe here all alone?" Aunt Laura asked.

"I'll be fine," Hartley assured them.

Hartley stood in the doorway and watched them drive away. As soon as she was sure they were gone, she ran upstairs to her bedroom. She found her old suitcase under her bed and began packing. She wasn't sure where she was going, but she knew she needed to get out of Cainsville for a while. She needed to figure out her plans and the best place to do that was anywhere but here. Hartley would be long gone before the tornado hit. She also would be traveling alone, so she knew her first vision couldn't come true.

She wrote a note explaining things to her aunt and uncle. She told them not to worry that she would be back soon. Hartley then took Bob Dylan and chained him in the storm cellar. Her golden retriever began to whimper when he realized she was leaving without him.

"I'm sorry, Bob, but I have to go. I'll come back. You'll be safe down here," Hartley promised the dog. She gave Bob a hug and kiss before leaving. Hartley grabbed her suitcase and walked out the front door where she collided with Tyler.

"What are you doing here?" Hartley asked Tyler, who was wearing a tux and holding a corsage presumably meant for her.

"Taking you to prom. Look, Hartley, I know you're mad, but you have to believe me. I didn't tell

159

any…" Tyler stopped when he realized Hartley was holding a suitcase.

"Are you going somewhere?" Tyler asked.

"I'm just going out for a little while," Hartley said.

"And that requires a suitcase?" Tyler asked. "You're running away, aren't you?"

"Maybe I am. What do you care?" Hartley asked.

"You can't run away, Hartley. What about the tornado and making sure everyone's safe?" Tyler asked.

"It's all taken care of. I have to go," Hartley said.

"I'll tell your aunt and uncle," Tyler threatened.

"Go ahead. I'll be long gone by the time you get there," Hartley said. She threw her suitcase in the back of her truck and drove off. She watched Tyler disappear from her rearview mirror and felt a tear slide down her face.

* * * * * * * * * * * * * * * * * * *

Hartley had been driving for a while when she topped the hill and saw a car with smoke coming out of the hood. As she got closer she realized she knew the car. There was only one person in Cainsville who drove a red convertible.

As she looked closer, Hartley saw Carmen standing beside her car, wearing a short, bright-orange prom dress. Hartley told herself not to stop. She considered hitting Carmen with her truck but decided to pull over instead.

"What are you doing out here?" Hartley asked Carmen.

"None of your business. Go away," Carmen said to Hartley.

"There's a storm coming. It's not safe out here. Get in the truck and I'll give you a ride," Hartley said, although she had no idea why she was offering.

"Like I would go anywhere with a freak like you," Carmen said. "I'll wait for the next car."

Hartley heard the rumble of thunder in the distance. Not a good sign. "There's not going to be another car this way. I'm the first person you've seen, in what? An hour? Get in the truck. We shouldn't be out here."

"NO," Carmen said firmly.

"Why are you out here, anyway?" Hartley asked.

"If you have to know, I was getting my hair and makeup done in the city," Carmen said.

"Why are you alone? Don't you usually do that kind of stuff with your friends?" Hartley asked curiously. She usually never saw Carmen without a couple of her friends flanking her.

"They all went out with their dates," Carmen said. "But I don't have a date because you stole my boyfriend!"

"I didn't steal your boyfriend. Besides, he wasn't a very good one. He told you all of my deep dark secrets the first chance he got," Hartley said. Carmen started laughing hysterically.

"What's wrong with you?" Hartley asked. She could hear the thunder getting closer.

"You actually believed that? Tyler didn't tell me anything. You did. I heard your pathetic confession in the library. I told the whole school so you would think it was Tyler. Then Tyler was supposed to ask me to prom and everything would be as it should." Carmen said.

"What kind of messed up person are you?" Hartley asked.

"I'm the messed up one? You're the freak who thinks she can see the future," Carmen said. Hartley saw a flash of lightning out of the corner of her eye.

"Whatever. I hope the tornado blows you away," Hartley said as she walked away.

"Run away, Hartley, like a little baby. Maybe the big bad twister will get you so you can be with your parents again, your stupid parents that got themselves killed by a tornado." Carmen mocked in a baby voice.

Carmen had hit Hartley's boiling point. Hartley turned around and punched Carmen right in the face. Hartley heard Carmen's nose make a crunching sound as it began to spew blood.

"You broke my nose! You...." Carmen screamed, but Hartley wasn't sure what she called her. At that moment a high pitched whistling sound mixed with a deafening roar filled their ears. Far off, Hartley watched the twister of her vision descend and begin destroying the open Kansas plains that surrounded them.

Hartley ran as quickly as she could to her truck, followed by Carmen. Hartley started the engine and slammed the accelerator with all her might. In the passenger seat, Carmen was screaming at the top of her lungs. Hartley looked in the rear view mirror and saw the beastly tornado gaining on them. She realized there was no way to out run it. She began searching for a safe place to hide. She noticed a drainage pipe a quarter mile up the road.

"Carmen!" Hartley had to yell so Carmen would stop screaming. "We can't out run this. Do you see that drainage pipe on the side of that hill?" Carmen nodded silently.

"We have to get down there. If we get inside that pipe we might have a chance. Do you understand?" Hartley asked.

"Yes," Carmen whimpered.

Hartley stopped the truck on top of the hill and started running to the bottom. She had just reached the drainage pipe when she heard a scream behind her. She turned around in time to see Carmen tripping in her five inch heels and go tumbling down the hill. Carmen was on the ground clutching her ankle. The tornado was extremely close to them now. Hartley was having trouble standing because of the forceful wind.

"Hartley, help!" Carmen screamed over the howl of the wind.

Hartley paused for a split second. She could get into the drainage pipe and be safe from the tornado. She didn't have to help Carmen. Why should she? Carmen had done nothing but make her life miserable. Would it be her fault if Carmen was blown away?

Hartley turned around and ran to Carmen. Hartley helped her to her feet and supported most of her weight as she limped toward the drainage pipe. The pipe was a few feet off the ground. The wind was getting stronger and Hartley knew they had to be fast if they had any chance of surviving.

Hartley helped boost Carmen into the pipe. Carmen turned around and offered her hand to Hartley. But the twister had already arrived. Hartley turned around in time to see a piece of debris fly straight at her, and then everything went dark.

164

Carmen watched in horror as Hartley fell to the ground and her body was engulfed by the tornado.

* * * * * * * * * * * * * * * * * *

Tyler arrived at school as prom was in full swing. The gym was packed with couples dancing, but he didn't care. He was too busy trying to find the Sawyers to tell them about Hartley. His search was stopped when Keisha blocked his view.

"Tyler, have you seen Hartley? I really need to talk to her," Keisha asked.

"Yeah, she ran away. I'm trying to find her aunt and uncle. Have you seen them?" Tyler asked.

"What? Are you serious? Why?" Keisha asked frantically.

"I think you know why. Can you really blame her?" Tyler said as he spotted the Sawyers monitoring the punch bowl.

Wyatt and Laura were talking to Mr. Pooler, waiting for the perfect time to sneak into the principal's office. They were surprised to see Tyler running toward them.

"Tyler, what's wrong?" Laura asked.

"It's Hartley. She ran away," Tyler said.

"What?" Laura and Wyatt yelled simultaneously.

"I stopped by your house. I was trying to convince her to go to prom with me, but she got in her truck and drove off. She wouldn't even tell me where she was going," Tyler said.

"We have to go find her," Wyatt said.

"What about the storm, Wyatt?" Laura asked.

"Don't worry; I'll take care of it," replied Mr. Pooler.

"I'll help," Tyler said.

"Me too," Keisha said joining the conversation.

"Thanks," Wyatt said as he and Laura ran toward the door.

"What do we do now?" Keisha asked. She was feeling guilty for the terrible things she said to Hartley. She had to make it up to her and was willing to help in any way possible.

"I'll go to the office and pull the alarm," Mr. Pooler explained. "It will look less suspicious if a teacher is caught in there. When you hear the alarm, make sure everyone gets into the locker room, understand?"

"Yeah," Tyler said.

A few minutes later they heard the alarm go off. Everyone began to panic, but Keisha and Tyler ushered everyone into the locker rooms. As the crowd crammed into the room, they heard the thunderous roar of wind as the twister plowed through the school. Some people were crying; while others were praying. It seemed as though the horrifying cyclone would never go away.

* * * * * * * * * * * * * * * * * *

As Wyatt and Laura left the school, "Where should we look first?" Laura asked.

"We should go to the sheriff. He can help us," Wyatt said.

The sky was starting to get dark and the wind was beginning to blow. They knew a storm was coming, and they had to act fast.

The police station wasn't far from the school. It was a slow night with only the Sheriff and one deputy working. Sheriff Jerry Jackson was surprised to see Laura and Wyatt Sawyer enter the police station looking rather disturbed.

"What can I do for you folks, tonight?" Sheriff Jackson asked.

"It's Hartley. She ran away from home," Laura explained.

"I'm sorry. Any idea where she's going?" asked the Sheriff.

"No idea," Wyatt said.

"Okay, stay calm. I can't put an alert out on her because she's eighteen and technically an adult. But, we'll all go out and look for her," Sheriff Jackson said.

At that very moment, the tornado hit the town. The sheriff and deputy ushered the Sawyers to the back of the station and into the jail cells. They spent what seemed like an eternity riding out the storm. Finally when the coast was clear, the four staggered out to survey the storm damage. What they saw shocked them. The Cainsville they knew was completely gone.

Chapter 15

Hartley felt the sun shining on her face, but she did not want to wake up. She was very comfortable staying asleep. She forced herself to open her eyes. She saw a beautiful blue sky full of fluffy white clouds and the sun gleaming brightly.

"I'm alive! I can't believe I survived!" Hartley exclaimed as she sat up. She realized she was in a strange field full of brilliant red poppies. Something sparkly at her feet made her look down. She was wearing her prom dress and on her feet were a pair of ruby red cowboy boots.

"Or maybe I didn't?" Hartley said as she continued to look around. There were flowers as far as she could see, except for a dazzling golden line zigzagging through the sea of red. As Hartley looked more closely, she realized it was a yellow brick road.

"I'm definitely not in Kansas, anymore," Hartley said.

Chapter 16

"Do you really think she'll be out here, Jerry?" Wyatt asked.

"It's where I found her seventeen years ago," the Sheriff simply said as he steered his patrol car in the direction of the Harper's field.

Night had fallen, and the sheriff and the Sawyers were out searching for Hartley. Their attempts were proving useless though. Carmen Guilden had been found safe, except for a broken nose and sprained ankle. She told the deputy that found her that Hartley had been swept away by the twister. The sheriff had a bad feeling; if Hartley had been picked up by the tornado, then there was only a very small chance of finding her alive. Sheriff Jackson reminded himself that Hartley had managed to survive the tornado that killed her parents. He hoped that she would be able to do it again.

The sheriff could tell the Sawyers were worried. They had searched half the county without any luck. The sheriff thought maybe Hartley would be in the same spot he found her all those years ago. As they arrived at Harper's field, they could tell that the tornado had torn through by the amount of debris scattered everywhere.

Sheriff Jackson gave Laura and Wyatt flashlights and they began their search. The three walked in different directions, carefully stepping over debris. The sheriff was about to give up when something caught his eye. It was Hartley lying face down on the ground. He yelled for the Sawyers. Her pulse was faint, but she was still breathing. He knew Hartley was seriously injured by the way her body was lying contorted on the ground. He told the Sawyers not to move her as he radioed for an ambulance. The sheriff hoped Hartley's time wasn't running out.

Chapter 17

Hartley had been walking for what felt like hours. Or was it minutes? Hartley had lost all sense of time. Her boots made a clicking sound with each step she took on the yellow brick road. Hartley wasn't sure if she was dreaming or if she was dead. She sincerely hoped it was the first option.

As she walked, Hartley admired the land around her. Once she got out of the flowers, the bright green fields surrounded by the brilliant blue sky were breathtaking. The yellow brick road winding through the middle of the landscape only added to the beauty.

Although she was surrounded by a picturesque landscape, Hartley still felt uneasy. She had the overwhelming desire to go home. She wanted to see her family again. The only problem was she wasn't sure how to get home.

She continued traveling for what seemed like miles when she arrived at a fork in the road. The golden path split in two directions, and there were no signs to guide her. She had no idea which road to take. Hartley was mad; she felt like yelling, so that is exactly what she did.

"Okay, God!" Hartley shouted to the sky. "I need some help here. I mean at least Dorothy had some help. She had a scarecrow, a tin man, a lion, and Toto! She also had a witch chasing her! I'll take anything! Even some flying monkeys! Help me, please!"

"We're no flying monkeys, but your mother can be a real witch when she's cranky," a voice from behind her said. "George!" a second voice scolded. Hartley was frozen in place. She hadn't heard those voices in seventeen years and was afraid if she turned around they wouldn't be real.

She took a deep breath before slowly turning. Hartley saw the most incredible sight in front of her.

"Mom? Dad?" Hartley gasped.

Chapter 18

"Last night, an F5 tornado hit the small town of Cainsville, Kansas, destroying everything in its path," The newswoman said. "It is being called a miracle. There were no causalities; however, one person was hospitalized and remains in critical condition."

"It was a miracle called Hartley," Tyler said angrily as the news report went off. He was in the hospital waiting room along with Keisha and Mr. Pooler. They were gathered waiting to hear news about Hartley.

"She's going to be okay, right? I mean she has to be okay," Keisha asked aloud.

"She's strong, she'll pull through," Mr. Pooler assured her, although he didn't sound so sure himself.

"Mind if I wait with you?" Carmen asked as she hobbled to the waiting area on crutches. She had a bandage across her nose.

"I thought you hated her," Keisha said.

"She saved my life; it's the least I can do," Carmen replied as she took her seat.

Laura and Wyatt waited in the hospital room to speak with the doctor. They knew Hartley was not doing well.

"She looks so small and fragile," Laura said as she held Hartley's hand. She was hooked up to IVs, a breathing tube, and had casts and bandages covering most of her body. Laura couldn't help the tears that were spilling from her eyes.

"I promised her I wouldn't let anything bad happen to her," Wyatt said guiltily.

"You can't blame yourself," Laura said.

"She's going to be alright." Wyatt started saying over and over, trying to convince himself it was true. Dr. Carpenter entered the room and immediately Laura and Wyatt started asking questions.

"Your niece sustained several serious injuries, including severe brain trauma," the doctor said.

"When will she wake up?" Laura asked.

"She is in a coma. It's the brain's way of healing itself. It's hard to say when she'll wake up or if she will wake up," Dr. Carpenter said.

"What? Isn't there anything else you can do?" Wyatt asked.

"You need to prepare yourselves. If your niece does wake up, she might not be the same person she was before," the doctor tried to explain.

"What do you mean?" Laura asked.

"Hartley is very lucky to be alive at this point. You need to brace yourselves for the possibility of life without her," the doctor said as he left the room.

"Please come back, Hartley, please," Laura and Wyatt begged.

Chapter 19

"Mom, Dad? Is it really you?" Hartley asked, as she stared in disbelief at the sight before her. George and Sarah Redfield looked exactly like they did in the photographs Hartley had of them.

"Yes, sweetheart, it's really us," Sarah said. Hartley stood there in awe. She wasn't sure if she could believe it. Hartley rushed forward and gave her parents the biggest hug she possibly could. As she felt their arms around her, she once again began to question whether she was alive.

"Am I dead?" Hartley blurted out. She must be if she was with her parents.

"No, you're not dead," George said.

Hartley was very glad to hear this news. However, she was still puzzled.

"If I'm not dead, are you alive?" Hartley asked hopefully. Maybe they had a shot of being a real family again.

"I'm afraid not," Sarah said sadly.

"Then where are we?" Hartley asked curiously.

"We're just meeting in the middle for a little while," George said.

Hartley sat down on the yellow brick road and began to cry. She couldn't control it. She had finally found her parents, and they were still dead.

"Don't cry, honey," Sarah said sitting down beside Hartley. George sat down on Hartley's other side and put his arm around her.

"My life is a mess. I ran away from home. I lost my boyfriend and my best friend. I didn't get into Stanford. I didn't even stick around to make sure everyone was safe. I'm a horrible person." Hartley confessed to her parents.

"You're not a horrible person." Her dad said.

"Really? Because I feel like one," Hartley asked doubtfully.

"You made sure you had a plan to keep everyone safe. You went back to help Carmen, even though she was awful to you. That shows you have a great deal of compassion for others," her mother explained.

"What about Tyler and Keisha and college?" Hartley asked.

"Your friends will come back, and you're way too young to date anyway," her dad said, making Hartley laugh.

"Didn't you date mom in high school?" Hartley asked her father.

"And you're way too smart," George joked.

"Apparently not smart enough for Stanford," Hartley said.

"Why did you want to go there?" Sarah asked her.

"To make you proud," Hartley said.

"We are proud of you, Hartley. Don't ever doubt that," Her mother said.

"Of course we are. We're proud of you no matter what," George said.

"Even if I don't go to college?" Hartley asked.

"We just want you to be happy," George said. Sarah nodded in agreement.

"Really?" Hartley asked.

"Really." Her parents said together.

They continued to talk for what felt like hours. Hartley was able to ask all the questions that she had been wondering about her entire life. When she eventually ran out of questions Hartley knew it was her time to be going home; she didn't belong there anymore.

"I should probably be getting back home. Aunt Laura and Uncle Wyatt might be worried." Hartley said. "But, I'm not ready to leave you."

"Sweetheart, we're always with you," Sarah explained.

"Even if you can't see us, we're always there," George said.

"I love you," Hartley said.

"We love you," they replied.

"How do I get back?" Hartley asked curiously. She had no idea how to get back home to Kansas.

"You know how the story ends, sweetheart," George said smiling at Hartley's shoes.

"Of course!" Hartley said. How could she have forgotten?

"There's no place like home," Hartley said, while clicking her heels together three times.

Her parents, along with the yellow brick road, slowly faded out of sight. Her parents waved goodbye as Hartley traveled back home where she belonged.

Chapter 20

It had been two weeks since the tornado had hit. The town was slowly rebuilding, but it was going to be a long time before Cainsville was back to normal. Hartley's condition remained unchanged. Mr. Pooler, Tyler, Keisha, and Carmen were all daily visitors. Her aunt and uncle rarely left her side. Fortunately, their farm had been spared from the destruction of the tornado.

Laura and Wyatt were sitting in the hospital room with Hartley. Laura was working on her sewing, and Wyatt was reading the newspaper. The only sound in the room was the gentle beeping of the heart monitor. The room was perfectly still, until a small movement caught Laura's attention.

"Wyatt," Laura said in a very serious tone.

"What's wrong?" asked Wyatt.

"Look at Hartley's feet," Laura said. Wyatt looked at the end of the bed where Hartley's feet were sticking out. She was tapping her heels together.

"Go get the doctor!" Laura said as Wyatt ran out of the room. He returned minutes later with the doctor and several nurses in tow.

"What's happening?" the doctor asked. Laura pointed to Hartley's moving feet. At that moment Hartley opened her eyes.

"Mmmmm," Hartley mumbled, but the breathing tube prevented her from talking.

The doctor removed the tube so Hartley could speak.

"What's going on? Where am I?" Hartley whispered hoarsely.

"You're in the hospital," Laura explained.

"You got caught in the tornado," Wyatt said.

The doctor and nurses began examining Hartley and asking if she was in pain. The truth was Hartley was hurting from her head to her toes. She looked down and noticed that she had an arm and leg in a cast. The other arm and leg were covered in scratches. She could feel bandages around her ribs, and it was very painful to breathe. Hartley also had a sharp pain radiating from her head.

The doctor began explaining that Hartley would have to stay in the hospital for a couple of days. The doctor also explained that Hartley might have some memory issues and experience some side effects due to the head injury. Hartley could remember everything, so she ruled out having memory issues. The side effects, however, did concern her.

The doctors and nurses finally left after instructing Hartley to get plenty of rest. But rest was the last thing Hartley wanted to do. She had a lot of questions and wanted answers.

"How long have I been out?" Hartley asked. She had no idea what day it was.

"Two weeks," Uncle Wyatt said.

"Two weeks?" Hartley asked. She thought maybe a couple of hours, not a couple of weeks. "Is everyone okay? How's Carmen?"

"Everyone is fine. Carmen has a sprained ankle and a broken nose, but other than that she's fine," Aunt Laura said.

"How's the town. Is the farm okay? Did you find Bob Dylan in the storm cellar?" Hartley asked, quickly avoiding the fact she was responsible for Carmen's broken nose.

"Bob Dylan is fine. Tyler's taking care of him. The farm is okay, the town not so much. The tornado pretty much leveled everything," Uncle Wyatt explained.

"Why did you run away, Hartley?" Aunt Laura asked.

"I don't know. I just wanted to get away for a little while. I never meant for all this to happen," Hartley said.

"We're glad you're safe, but you're grounded for a month for scaring us to death," Uncle Wyatt said.

Hartley laughed and said, "That's okay, I deserve it. I don't think I'll be running anytime soon anyway." She had never been grounded before, so there was a first time for everything. She decided to keep seeing her parents a secret. She didn't want to scare her aunt and uncle by telling them she had a conversation with her dead parents.

Hartley had to stay in the hospital for another week. She was surprised at how many visitors she had, including her fellow classmates who came to apologize. The visitor that surprised her most, however, was Carmen.

Hartley was resting in bed when Carmen came into the room. Aunt Laura, who had been sitting with Hartley, left the room to give them some privacy.

"Hi," Hartley said.

"Hi," Carmen replied.

"I'm sorry about…." Hartley said pointing the large bandage covering Carmen's nose.

"Don't worry about it. I've been wanting an excuse to get it redone," Carmen said.

Hartley started laughing, but stopped due to the pain. "Don't make me laugh! It hurts too much."

"Look, Hartley, I wanted to say how sorry I am about everything. I know I've given you a hard time over the years, and you didn't deserve it. Nobody deserves to be treated the way I treated you," Carmen said.

"I'm not going to lie. I really hated you for a long time," Hartley said.

"Why did you save my life then?" Carmen asked.

"No one deserves to die like that, not even you," Hartley said.

"The truth is... I was jealous of you. You were everything I wasn't. Smart. Nice. You were so close with Tyler. It was easier for me to be mean to you," Carmen confessed.

"It's okay. All this..." Hartley said pointing to her many bandages and casts, "has really put things in perspective for me. Life is too short for us to spend hating each other. Maybe we can start over? Forget everything. I mean, we're about to leave for college and probably won't see each other for a couple years, so it should be easy."

"Thank you," Carmen said as she hugged Hartley.

"Ow," Hartley said pushing her away.

"Too soon?" Carmen asked, looking hurt.

"No. I just broke most of my ribs. It's really painful," Hartley said.

"Oh, I almost forgot," Carmen said, pulling something out of her bag and handing it to Hartley. It was a plastic tiara.

"Oh, wow, you shouldn't have?" Hartley said questioningly.

"Our class decided that you should be the prom queen, since you saved all our lives," Carmen explained. "The real crown got destroyed and this was all we could find."

"That's nice. Tell everyone thanks for me," Hartley said. It was a really nice gesture although she should have known the only way she would be prom queen was if a disaster happened.

"I will. Bye, Hartley," Carmen said as she left the room. She had only been gone a few moments when Tyler and Keisha appeared.

Keisha ran forward and gave Hartley a big hug. Hartley suffered through the pain for the sake of her friend.

"I'm so glad you're okay. I was so worried! I'm sorry for everything I said before. Please don't be mad at me," Keisha blurted out in one breath.

"It's okay, Keisha, I'm not mad. You were right. I should have told you the truth," Hartley said.

"No. I was wrong. The more I thought about it, you were right not to tell me. I so could not have handled it," Keisha said.

Hartley noticed Tyler was standing in the back, not saying a word.

"Keisha, I'm feeling kind of sleepy. Could you go find me some coffee, please?" Hartley asked, looking for an excuse to be alone with Tyler.

"You got it. Anything you want. I'll be right back," Keisha said leaving the room.

"Hey," Hartley said to Tyler as she motioned for him to sit next to her.

"How are you feeling?" Tyler asked as he sat down.

"I've been better," Hartley said. "I'm sorry for not believing you. You gave me no reason not to trust you. I guess it was easier for me to believe that you would choose Carmen over me."

"That's ridiculous, I will always choose you," Tyler said, making Hartley smile. "I still have no idea how she found out, though."

"She was spying on us in the library that day. She heard me say everything," Hartley said.

"What? I can't believe she would do that," Tyler said angrily.

"Yeah. I punched her in the face when I found out," Hartley bragged.

Tyler started laughing. "You did that? She told everyone it happened during the tornado."

"Technically it did," Hartley said.

"I'm glad you're okay. I was afraid you wouldn't make it," Tyler said.

"Really? How worried were you?" Hartley asked.

"I was worried I would never be able to do this again," Tyler said as he leaned over to kiss Hartley lightly on the lips.

They were interrupted by a knock on the door. Tyler and Hartley looked up to see Mr. Poolcr laughing at them. Both their faces turned bright red.

"I was going to ask if you were feeling better, but I can see that you are," Mr. Pooler said jokingly.

"We can't catch a break can we?" Tyler whispered to Hartley then said, "I think I'll go help Keisha with that coffee," as he left the room.

"So sorry to interrupt, but I brought you a present," Mr. Pooler told Hartley as he sat in the chair next to her bed.

"I was already named prom queen and received this lovely crown today. It's going to be hard to beat that," Hartley joked.

"Oh, I think you'll like this," Mr. Pooler said as he handed Hartley an envelope.

Hartley took the envelope with her one good hand, but couldn't open it.

"A little help?" Hartley asked.

"Sorry," Mr. Pooler said as he opened the envelope and unfolded the letter for her to read.

The letter was from the University of Oklahoma and read: "We are pleased to inform you that you are the lucky recipient of the University of Oklahoma Atmospheric Science Scholarship."

"I got it?" Hartley asked in disbelief. She remembered sending in her application but never thought she actually had a shot.

"You got it," Mr. Pooler said.

"I can't believe it," Hartley said.

"I know this wasn't your first choice Hartley, but it's a good opportunity," Mr. Pooler said.

"I didn't get into Stanford," Hartley informed Mr. Pooler as she continued to read the letter.

"I'm sorry. I know how much you wanted to go there," Mr. Pooler said.

"I think you were right, Mr. Pooler," Hartley said.

"Right about what?" Mr. Pooler asked curiously.

"Right about how I shouldn't plan my future because I never know what's going to happen," Hartley explained. "I think there might be something to that."

"So you're going to study meteorology at the University of Oklahoma?" Mr. Pooler asked.

"Yeah, I think so," Hartley said nodding her head. "Ironic, huh?"

They laughed, and for the first time in a long time, Hartley felt okay about her future. She had a feeling that she was doing the right thing. She had planned on being a doctor and helping people, but maybe she could be a meteorologist and help people. Maybe she could find a new way to save lives.

Hartley was happy to finally be released from the hospital. The doctor warned her to take it slow. Hartley was positive that slow was the only speed she could go. She still had to wear a cast on her left leg and right arm. She had figured out how to walk with one crutch, but only at snail's pace. Her ribs were still sore, but with the exception of an occasional headache, she was back to normal. Almost.

Hartley had a feeling her visions were gone for good. Her theory hadn't been tested, since there had not been another tornado. Deep down she knew they were gone. Hartley wasn't complaining. She had been dreaming of being normal her entire life. Now that she had the opportunity, she wasn't sure how to adjust. What if people died because her visions were gone? She had this discussion with Aunt Laura and Uncle Wyatt when she arrived home from the hospital.

Hartley was resting on the couch, with Bob Dylan standing guard at her side. Her loyal dog had not left her side since she came home. Hartley assumed Bob had forgiven her for locking him in the storm cellar.

The whole family was watching the weather report on the local news. The weather man warned several counties to watch for severe weather the following week. Both Aunt Laura and Uncle Wyatt looked to Hartley as if she might have some knowledge on the subject.

"I think my visions are gone," Hartley said.

"Gone for good?" Uncle Wyatt asked.

"Yeah, I think so," Hartley sighed.

"Isn't that what you wanted?" Aunt Laura asked.

"Yes, but what if someone dies or gets hurt because I don't have a vision," Hartley said. "I don't want anyone to die because of me."

"Hartley, you can't think like that. It is not your responsibility to personally save every single tornado victim," Aunt Laura told her.

"It feels like it is," Hartley confessed.

"The fact that you are feeling guilty about getting the chance to be normal is proof of what a good person you are," Uncle Wyatt told her.

"You can't worry about everyone, Hartley," Aunt Laura said.

"I guess you're right. I'll just have to adjust," Hartley told them.

"You'll still help people, Hartley," Her aunt and uncle told her.

"How?" Hartley asked, wondering how they knew that.

"You'll figure it out. We know you will."

Chapter 21

Graduation day finally arrived. School had been canceled after the tornado hit, mainly because the school had been destroyed. The next month had been spent rebuilding the town which was progressing greatly every day.

The graduation ceremony was being held on a makeshift stage on what once was the football field. The graduating class sat proudly in their red robes and caps. Hartley tried to calm her nerves as she prepared to give her speech. She took a deep breath as Principal Burns introduced her as the class valedictorian. Hartley refused to deliver her speech sitting down, so she balanced on her good leg while holding onto the podium for support.

"Many of you have heard the expression, 'When one door closes, another door opens.'" Hartley began her speech and continued, "I had never really given this expression much thought until recently. Now, I realize how true it is and how it applies to every aspect of my life. It applies to my family, my school, and even my friends."

"When my parents died seventeen years ago, I lost the chance of having a normal family: a mom, a dad, brothers, sisters. But when that door closed, I was given the opportunity to live with two of the most amazing people. They have given me nothing but love and happiness. They have helped shape the person I have become today, and for that I owe them everything," Hartley paused to look into the audience for Aunt Laura and Uncle Wyatt. She found them both smiling and crying simultaneously. She continued with her speech.

"I always dreamed of going to Stanford University, my parents' alma mater, and becoming a doctor. The part that attracted me most was the sunny California weather and the lack of tornadoes." The audience laughed with her. "But that door was abruptly slammed shut a few weeks ago when I opened my rejection letter. I thought my college dream was over before it had even begun." She paused a moment before continuing. "With a little help from a great teacher," Hartley nodded to Mr. Pooler who smiled in response, "I realized the possibility of a new dream. A new door was opened for me. I am happy to say that this fall I will be attending the University of Oklahoma to study atmospheric science. I know the irony is not lost on all of you." She had the audience laughing again.

"I spent much of my high school career hating most of my fellow classmates, one in particular. She did a really fantastic job of making my life miserable," Hartley said as she looked at Carmen. Carmen was smiling at her. "It took us nearly dying to realize maybe we could put our differences aside and be friends. When I closed the door to hatred, the door to friendship opened up."

"Now the door to high school is closing. As we say goodbye to our families, friends, teachers, and our town, a new door is opening for all of us, the door to our future. I don't know what the future has in store, but I do know the possibilities are endless. Remember when one door closes, another better door will always open." Hartley finished her speech and the audience erupted in applause. Hartley took a second to appreciate the moment. She had made it through high school, something she had always thought was impossible. Hartley had a feeling her life was only going to get better.

* * * * * * * * * * * * * * * * * *

The summer flew by. Hartley had unfortunately spent most of it in physical therapy learning to use her arm and leg again. Having her boyfriend to help her through it made it much better. Tyler had been by her side practically the whole summer, and Hartley wasn't complaining. They were both excited to start college, especially since they were going to the same one. When the day finally came for them to leave, Hartley was more emotional than she thought she would be.

"Are you sure you have everything?" Aunt Laura asked for the fifteenth time.

"Yes," Hartley replied putting another box in Tyler's car. Her truck was a victim of the tornado. After two months, they still hadn't found it. Since Hartley got a scholarship, she was planning on using the money she had saved to buy a new one. Until she did, she was carpooling with Tyler.

"Hurry up, Hartley!" Keisha yelled from the backseat. Keisha's plans of moving in with her grandma in Chicago were dashed when her grandma moved in with her mom in Cainsville. Keisha decided to go to OU with Hartley and be her roommate.

"You know this would go faster if you actually helped," Hartley said.

"You know I would, but I won't," Keisha said. Hartley rolled her eyes. College was going to be interesting. Hartley walked back up the steps to say goodbye to her aunt and uncle.

"Be safe," Uncle Wyatt said.

"I will," Hartley said.

"Remember to call," Her aunt said.

"I will. I will also be home every weekend so don't get to comfy living without me," Hartley said.

"We wouldn't dream of it," Aunt Laura replied.

"Don't do drugs," Uncle Wyatt added.

"I won't," Hartley said laughing.

"We'll miss you," Aunt Laura and Uncle Wyatt said giving Hartley a giant hug.

"I'll miss you too," Hartley said. Bob Dylan started barking. Hartley sat down beside him and gave him a hug.

"Of course I'm going to miss you too, Bob," Hartley said. "Next year, I'll get my own place and you can come live with me," Hartley said, reassuring her golden retriever.

"Hartley, are you ready to go?" Tyler asked as he put the last box in the car.

"Yeah, just a minute," Hartley said as she looked at her aunt and uncle. They smiled at her and said, "We love you."

"I love you too," Hartley said. "I'll see you next weekend." Aunt Laura and Uncle Wyatt smiled as she said that.

She smiled as she got in the passenger seat. Tyler started the car and they drove away. Hartley waved goodbye one final time and smiled as she closed one door and a new one opened.

Made in the USA
Charleston, SC
07 June 2014